Nicked Names

Andrew Geoffrey Kwabena Moss

First Published: 2022

10 9 8 7 6 5 4 3 2 1

ISBN 978-0-6454326-2-6

Printed & Bound in Australia

Published by RoseyRavelston Books

roseyravelstonbooks.com

For Peter John Moss

'Language is the very opposite of violence...

...the means the group provides itself with

to maintain power outside coercive violence;

as the guarantee repeated daily

that this threat is averted.'

-Pierre Clastres

CHAPTER ONE

Welcome to Blandfordshire
- A Progressive County

'Welcome to Blandfordshire – A Progressive county' read the black and white sign on entry to Blandford, the bland 'meat and two veg' town where Norman 'Zebra' Smith lived. Whenever Norman returned to his hometown after escaping by car, the sign that it was a 'progressive county' reminded him of the irony.

Blandford was the first, or last, town in the county, depending on which direction you were travelling in. In the direction of Norman's life, it was a last resort. Because of its place in the world, Blandford seemed to feel the need to make a statement. It was a town that in Norman's eyes rested not on its ley lines but its metaphorical fault lines.

'What does progressive mean?' Norman asked his father, nodding casually towards the sign beyond the raindrop-speckled car window.

'Progressive, in this case, is used as an adjective, not a noun…' began Mr Smith as he held his horn-rimmed glasses by the top right corner. He always did this when he was about to become involved in a discussion.

His Dad was an English teacher at Blandford's

prestigious former grammar school, Redwood Glade Secondary. When it came to language, his standards were always exacting. Norman attended the less salubrious Brookdale Upper School at the other end of town. His mother and Norman had conspired to ensure that he went there, for fear that his father's eccentricities would make school life even harder for him.

'Come on Dad,' replied Norman impatiently. He wanted the direct route to the answer on this occasion, not the scenic one.

'In the context of that particular sign, 'progressive' means the county is growing, increasing, developing, getting better, stronger.' Norman's dad punctuated his point with a conductor's flourish; a light, upward flick of the indicator lever.

Norman smiled. He admired his dad's talents as a walking dictionary, encyclopaedia and thesaurus rolled into one. Mr Smith was faster than Google. There was no risk of RSI or eyestrain from typing and squinting at a phone; no download limits or buffering to worry about. It saved a lot of time looking up words for Year 10 assignments.

Norman, with his father's enthusiastic encouragement, grew up intrigued by words and their shades of meaning.

'Why do you think they write that on the sign, Norman?' quizzed his dad, a Socratic gadfly initiating cerebral challenges. Mr Smith relished questioning his son about words to develop his understanding, or, as he termed it 'grazing in semantic fields, cowed by the might of the English language.' Making obscure puns was another Smith trademark.

'Probably, I guess…to encourage people to come here or live here,' ventured Norman. 'They're hardly going to write that it's a crap town, in a crap county.' Norman paused to think of a punchline. 'Blandford, the turd in its crown.'

'Indeed, quite right, Norman. Less Anglo-Saxon diction might become you, however, although that's what the graffiti may say…but I do appreciate your extended faecal metaphor,' chuckled his dad.

Buoyed by his father's willingness to listen and validate him, Norman continued. 'Blandford doesn't seem progressive to me. Things here don't change much. It's a middle-class market town in Middle England with old people, old churches and old windmills.'

'It was an interesting and heartfelt observation, Norman. That's the thing about words. You need to question the message behind them – test them.'

Norman's dad encouraged his son's critical thinking at every opportunity. Mr Smith turned up 'Classic FM' on the radio for full appreciation of the harpsichord.

To say Blandford was dull was to do a disservice to the word 'dull'. The highlight of the year in this conservative enclave was the dance around the maypole at the Recreation Ground. With the exception of its outdoor pool, empty on Health and Safety grounds, it was a picture postcard framed with a Victorian bandstand. There were scones, coconut shies, pony treks and homemade jam stalls without a Caribbean steel pan in sight. It was a land of Neighbourhood Watch, twitching net curtains and local newspaper headlines about stuck-up residents and cats stuck up trees.

Blandford boasted the most obscure claims to fame, which often caused bemusement, disappointment or embarrassment to teenagers vying for a place in 'Cool Britannia'. It was the town with the narrowest-gauge railway, the starting point of a narrow canal (narrow water for narrow boats to travel on) and, in Norman's eyes, a harbour for even narrower minds. Blandford was referred to in the Domesday Book, but to Norman it was just...doomed. To him, it felt as if it was stuck in 1086, not 2016.

Arguably the only exciting thing that ever happened there was the 1963 Great Train Heist, just outside Blandford. The perpetrators, like Norman, couldn't wait to escape. At least the train robbers managed to keep most of the £2.6 million, whereas Norman was sentenced to live in Blandford for the rest of his (school) life.

As soon as you confided to someone from outside Blandford about the name of the town where you lived, their eyes glazed over. They couldn't see past the prefix

'Bland'. Conspiratorially, the suffix 'ford' had been scribbled out with marker-pen on Stop 33 at the town centre bus station. Norman had always seen this as apt use of poetic licence because commuters heading through the dormitory to the more exciting and 'woke' destination of Leestone had their thoughts confirmed in signage.

Norman fondly remembered the smell of freshly fried plantain, the yams the size of bowling pins and the iridescence of tilapia fish that sparkled like treasure at Leestone's Afro-Caribbean markets. It had been strange yet comforting to see so many brown faces there. His family used to shop in Leestone before larger supermarkets had opened in Blandford, as it expanded to feed the growing number of affordably housed residents.

The ethereal exoticism was heightened, literally, by the kitsch yet somehow alluring gymnastic pyramid of plastic pink flamingos standing on top of each other. Jets of reflected shop sign neon-tinged water soothed the flamingos' webbed feet amid bronze and silver coins tossed into the shallow pool beneath them, tossed in dreams of escaping Leestone and striking it lucky with a National Lottery win to Torremolinos or the Costa del Sol. The tawdry eyesore performed a very necessary function though, as meeting place and beacon for myopic lovers and lost children alike.

Since Mr Smith reluctantly began the role of Deputy Head at Redwood Glade, the family had much less time for food shopping out of town. The Smiths were time-poor yet rich in corner shop convenience and the ephemera of takeaway.

Norman also thought back to the times when his dad had tried to make Blandford seem interesting by telling him how the name Blandford derived from the Old English 'bl-dge' (the inner vowel remained a mystery to linguists), and probably meant a ford where blay, a fish also known as the common bleak or gudgeon, swam.

But Norman himself was floundering, a fish out of water.

Jaded by the sound of violins caterwauling on the radio, Norman plugged back into his Hip-Hop fuelled iPod Classic. He preferred the scratching of records to the screeches of strings. Norman turned the device's click-wheel to be illuminated by choices. Giddy Vandal rapped above and beyond Grieg, followed by the Renowned L.I.T.T.L.E, surpassing Rachmaninoff. He favoured old skool electro beats, breakdance and linoleum to Elgar, Brahms or Liszt.

Father and son continued their journey past the sign and through the leafy outskirts of Blandford. Houses edged nearer together, hedgerows bunched ever closer and mansions gave way to semi-detached and terraced rows. Satellite dishes increased in size and number as they arrived at their neat but modest post-war semi-detached house. It was situated near the concrete and glass of the 1960s shopping precinct that sat uneasily near the 15th-century pentagonal Market Cross where the town's three oldest streets converged.

Their navy-blue Ford Granada entered the slender driveway, squeezing between the six-foot conifer sentinels. Their feathery fingertips shivered in the late afternoon breeze. The waxy and scaly needles somehow reminded Norman of seaweed and trips to the Cornish coast. Norman's father had installed them as a buffer against the blighted view of Mr Ariss's HGV lorry opposite. The brown and orange tractor head proudly announced MAN in metallic capitals on its radiator. Unfortunately, the fir barrier lacked the sound-absorbing qualities to counteract the 5am engine spluttering and choking as it warmed up for long-distance haulage duties.

Norman's dad opened the frosted glass and uPVC door. Lichen speckled the rubbery transoms. They were met on the porch by the melodramatic drumbeats that signalled the start of Norman's mum's soap opera viewing. His dad proceeded along the peach-coloured hallway and made a beeline to open the plastic faux mahogany concertina doors, the gateway to their galley kitchen. 'We're back, fancy a cuppa darling?'

'That would be lovely da',' replied Norman's mum.

The wallpaper bubbled underneath like a cross-section of an Aero bar. Norman popped his head around the living room door and his eyes met his mum's broad warm smile. Her gaze returned to the EastEnders inner-city map, awaiting her favourite Cockney characters, the regulars and extras at the Queen Vic.

Pressing down on the heels of his sports shoes, he replaced them with the familiar warmth of his lambswool-lined moccasins that sat at the foot of the purple English-rolled arm sofa. The worn shiny soles allowed him to skate on the Axminster carpet back towards the door. He passed the 1920s Asante Art Deco carved elephant stool in the hallway corner that carried their telephone, directories and Yellow Pages on its curved seat. The proverb came back to him 'when an elephant steps on a trap, it doesn't spring' and Norman mused momentarily on African wisdom.

Gripping to the snail shell spiral newel cap, Norman hoisted himself up the staircase. He gained purchase on the silky, thick enamel paint of the handrail to achieve momentum. Norman bounded past framed Adinkra symbols, a bright acrylic canvas of a tro tro with an 'In God We Trust' roof canopy sign and a wooden Benin mask that leaned diagonally like exotic flying duck hangings. His bedroom door still had the ceramic tile with his name in capital double line lettering above a vintage racing car.

His right trouser leg brushed against the xylophone-ribbed radiator that was precariously attached to the wall. Norman reached up with his left hand to press the standby button of his 14" Matsui TV that jutted out from the L-shaped extendable wall bracket arm. With a perfect ten muscle memory score, he launched himself backwards onto his bed and sighed with satisfaction.

Dominating the right corner of the box room, protruded

a boiler enclosed in shiny white melamine. The immersion heater power point sat above it. Norman had filled this tabula rasa with images held fast with generous blobs of blu-tac to resist the warmth. Ripped pages of the portraits of Bob Marley, Pete Tosh, Big Youth and Augustus Pablo rubbed jagged shoulders with American civil rights leaders, MLK, Malcolm X and US rap stars.

Norman gazed up at the World Snooker Championships and relaxed into the rhythm of red and other coloured spheres rolling on baize, sinking into leather cushioned string pockets. Soothed by the commentator's husky voice and the kissing of phenolic resin, he was awoken abruptly.

'Dinner's ready Norm!' The evening rituals continued in familiar rhythm: washing up, homework and then a bath before bed.

At 6am the following morning the alarm went off. Norman smothered its high-pitched beeping with his pillow. When Norman realized it was Thursday morning, he rose with blurry eyes and more enthusiasm than usual to do his daily paper round.

On Thursdays, his favourite magazine, 'Hip Hop Connections', announced itself boldly on the shelves of the suburban shops. It was glossy and colourful in comparison to the other prosaic titles such as 'Woman's Own', 'The Radio Times', 'Countryfile' and 'Angler's

Weekly'. Norman eagerly anticipated opening the crisp pages, still sticky and smelling of printer's ink. He dreamt of escaping Blandford to enter The Bronx River Houses Project. From a safe voyeuristic distance, Norman liked to think of himself as an intrepid participant, an observer of cultural anthropology. Norman's only camouflage was that he shared a skin tone that could blend into those environs, though his accent would have quickly betrayed his alien status.

Norman was obsessed with the rhythm and language of rap music. Always a keen student, he was impressed, if not initially shocked, when his English teacher Ms Evens included 'rap' as a form of poetry on their Year 7 syllabus two years previously. Norman continued to research the genre and listened enthusiastically to a wide range of its repertoire.

He was especially attracted to the African American rappers, many of whom looked like him. Norman favoured the political message of 'knowledge rap' over the simplicity and dubious morality of 'gangsta'. To Norman, 'gangsta' was a form of minstrelsy; putting on a 'face' for commercialisation. Lyrics about black consciousness were preferable and easier to relate to than guns, women and money, all of which were in short supply in Blandford.

Norman eased himself out of bed like an injured sleepwalker staggering sideways to gather his bearings and then straightening up, like a dismounting gymnast to the challenges of the day. He got dressed in the half-light of dawn. With a fluorescent orange bag slung over his left shoulder, he finalised his ritual of intent before closing the door quietly so as not to wake up his parents. It was a brightly shocking reflection of Norman's status as wage slave; a cog in the chain of capitalism.

He cycled his rusty Raleigh BMX past Sandeep's Corner Shop, across the dimly lit Hickliffe Road and rebelliously entered the pedestrianized town centre towards Regency Street Newsagency. The moist tarmac kissed his tyres: the gentle smacking sound of shallow puddles awakened under the amber glow of sentinel streetlights. A familiar sprinkling of dirt on his back sent shivers up and down his spine; mudguards were not in vogue for BMX bandits.

Norman loved the peace of this time of day. There were fewer cars, less noise and fewer people but more time to just be and think.

He was alone with his thoughts, happily freewheeling as the winter sun struggled to force open the slate-grey clouds, when he saw it.

'GOLLIWOGS OUT' warned the graffiti sprayed on the exhaust-stained pebble-dashed wall of the Co-Op department store. The shock of the metallic blue words hit Norman hard. It was a bold and belligerent sign in broadening daylight. His feet stuck to the pedals; his eyes glued to the wall.

Norman, the child of a Ghanaian mother and English father, felt as if he was being warned directly. He thought back to when, at the age of five, he realised that the characters on his Nan's marmalade jars were not quite what they seemed, dressed up in suits with pinstriped trousers and wide-eyed smiles.

'Breakfast Victim', a rap he had recently written about this trauma came to him in an instant.

High over the fence jumped Sonny Jim
Forced was the food that raised him
Erased by Golliwogs on jam jar lids
All wide-eyed grins and vacant smiles
He was a marginalised victim.

There were implications that young minds were sensitive. Simplistic caricatures of an African family in the old-fashioned picture book 'Little Black Sambo'. Herge's natives with bones through their noses. And his grandmother's smirks at black and white minstrel shows. All provided puzzling clues.

Abruptly woken out of his daze by the beeping of a reversing delivery lorry, Norman's heart raced and synchronised with it. Was his sort welcome in Blandford?

Blandford was a largely monocultural town except for a handful of Pakistani, West Indian, Italian, Polish and Chinese families. None of these groups was large enough to be called a minority nor unified enough to be termed a community. In an era of state-sanctioned and sponsored multiculturalism in inner-cities, Blandford adhered to an old-fashioned conservative brand of assimilation or suspicion.

Norman had occasionally been given uncomfortable reminders, like the one on the wall that morning, that he was part of this group from 'elsewhere'. All Norman wanted to do was 'fit in'. Now, more keenly than ever, he felt like an outcast.

CHAPTER TWO

At the Margins
- School Rules

Over the coming days, the graffiti spread through all his thoughts. Mistrust and confusion besmirched his mind. Norman wondered if there was much difference between the writing on the wall that morning and the casual racism of microaggressions that he experienced every day. He spent the next week thinking about his precarious position in Blandford.

Norman 'Zebra' Smith was a thirteen-year-old misfit in the claustrophobic market town of Blandford. He earned his 'stripes' of distinction from his exotic background. He was of mixed African and European heritage, and he shared those features on his face. He had his father's angular Roman nose, Pictish freckles and dark green almond eyes. From his Ghanaian mother came the golden-brown, wiry, afro-textured hair that crowned his head in gravity-defying spirals. His skin was a reddish caramel blend of both worlds.

Norman turned heads as well as shifting continents closer together. The residents of Blandford were often uncertain of where he came from.

Apart from his mother, Norman was one of the few representatives of both the mixed-race community and the Afro-Caribbean community. To complicate matters further, due to his exotic looks he also passed for other ethnicities, and had at different times earned the dubious titles of 'Paki', 'I-Tie', 'Spic', 'Dago' or 'Chinky Chinese' to name but a few. As a result, at school, Norman felt he had more names than the United Nations. He represented the blurred line between familiarity and safety, living in a liminal landscape that could shift as quickly and uncertainly as sand.

How he wished for things to be less black and white. Norman wanted to be compared to a swatch of opulent Caribbean colours; the richer, poetic and sensory descriptions of 'high yellow' or reddish-brown rather than Blandford's black and white myopia. After all, thought Norman, the Inuits had fifty words for snow, Hawaiians had sixty words for wave and two hundred words for rain. It wasn't beyond the human capacity of imagination.

Norman loved language, but it was often used creatively against him. 'Oreo', 'Bounty Boy' and 'Zebra' were names - terms of endangerment to him - often used by students who didn't know what he was called or simply didn't know better. His minority 'status' marked him out for special treatment, whether he liked it or not.

'Hey Zebra, mind out! It's a zebra crossing!' teased one of the Year 8 students at the head of a pack of boys that boisterously raced past Norman, who had once again been lost in his thoughts. This was a regular quip that Norman endured. The group knocked past him cheerfully, rucksacks slung over shoulders, looking like they were only partially evolved from Neanderthals with clubs, or at best hunters with rabbits.

The flood gates had been opened. They happily put behind them the late 1960s blonde-brick Lego building that resembled an aircraft hangar. Its two-storey roofline sloped gradually to the right before plateauing to meet the overcast sky. Its façade was an off-centre section of floor-to-roof glass windows, separated by panels in the school colours of royal blue. It resembled the front of a greenhouse. Within its windows, students were hot-housed for educational 'success'. Quality was measured in league tables and the number of free school meals.

The Office for Standards in Education report soundbites were offered on the school billboard, prospectus and other promotional material, to satiate statistically hungry consumers. In contrast to Redwood Glade, it was only deemed 'satisfactory' in its Victorian factory production line of education for the masses, neat rows of tables and tatty 20th-century textbooks lacking spines.

Originally, Brookdale Upper School had opened in 1959 as a shiny purpose-built institution, the result of a merger of two local boys' and girls' secondary modern schools. In those days Secondary Moderns taught a more skills-based curriculum, intended to fit pupils for a life of work rather than Redwood Glade's 'outstanding' Ofsted-endorsed emphasis on more academic subjects, with a view to pupils going on to attend university.

At the end of the 1960s, any selection to school was abandoned and replaced with a curriculum solely based on age. Blandford County Council supported the scheme and reorganized its school system accordingly. By the end of the 1970s, Brookdale was a fully-fledged Comprehensive High School for nine to seventeen-year-olds, with modern aspirations. In some ways, it was a beacon to a bygone era of social democratic educational reform. This history was little known to its 'customers', or social media observers; the haters and trolls of the 'Rate My Teacher' system.

In response to the air-raid siren that signalled 3:30pm, students who had slouched their way through the last lesson of the day now jumped up, like marlin loosening educational fishhooks. Norman was feeling less energetic.

Unlike most of the fish streaming home that afternoon, Norman felt like a minnow swimming against the current of indifference to his plight. The graffiti, the nicknames and the rucksacks pushed past him and knocked his already dented confidence.

Norman rounded the iron-spiked security railings, selectively streaked by the local pigeon population at the corner of the school. Edging out of sight of the CCTV cameras, Norman managed to shake off the crowd and steadied himself to his own pace. He heard footsteps in staccato behind him.

'Wait up. What's up?' asked his best friend Steve Euston in uncertain rising intonation. Norman stopped in his tracks and waited for Steve to bend forward and anchor his hands to his knees in a bid to regain his breath.

Steve and Norman had a bond founded on shared experience. 'Birds of a feather fly higher together,' Norman's dad had remarked about their friendship. Mr Smith liked to adapt aphorisms for his own amusement.

Norman and Steve had been mates since Clipcobble Brook Lower School. Norman had immediately and intuitively understood Steve as another 'oddity'. Steve was, and always would be, the shortest kid in the school. Quite possibly this would be the case in any school he attended. He only came up to Norman's underarms (and Norman was slightly under average height), owing to a lack of growth hormone production. Steve had confided in Norman that he had to visit the hospital regularly to have growth hormone injections.

One afternoon, several years ago when they were in Year 4, Steve had tentatively given Norman the last piece of the mysterious jigsaw.

'Norman, the reason I'm short is that...I've got...I've...got...only...one...ball.'

Norman felt at once a curious mixture of amusement, pity and understanding. He was uncertain whether to laugh, cry or pat Steve on the back. Acceptance was one thing he prided himself on. He always vowed to show people a tolerance for being different on the surface that others did not show him. Norman always championed the underdog, the Sambos, the jam jar figures of condescension. His mission was to describe nuance precisely, a luxury rarely granted to him. Whilst many of his classmates referred to Indian sub-continentals as Pakis, Norman preferred the precision of Bangladeshi or Sylheti, Indian or Pakistani. As a counterpoint, Norman used 'Stani' as an abbreviation.

He thought and searched for the right words to share with Steve.

'Look mate, who cares? They call me Zebra, it could be worse. You've got plenty of balls as far as I'm concerned!'

Norman and Steve comforted and strengthened each other by sharing their own vulnerability. Somehow their fears and worries, as soon as they were put into words, became less fearsome and worrisome. They had become great friends. The pals understood and trusted each other. Steve's nicknames 'Shorty', 'Micro' and 'Mini-me' were as commonplace, tedious and diminutive as Norman's.

Now it was Norman's turn to reveal part of his puzzle to Steve.

As they reached Steve's house on the corner of the leafy Otterbury Avenue, they sat down on the kerb, as was their habit at the end of their journey back home from school. The road ran parallel to Norman's but was effectively a parallel universe of expansive, new-build detached houses and landscaped gardens. It formed the boundary of Blandford's attempt to create aspirational estates. Often, they had too little time to analyse the day's events on the way home.

The sole of Norman's shoe rolled a twig rhythmically on the pavement. Nervous tension built between them. Finally, Norman's resolve broke at the snapping of the miniature tree limb.

'I'm sick of it mate. Always being the odd one out. I wish I didn't live in Blandford.'

Norman spat the words out with contempt as he looked down and scuffed loose gravel into the grill of the drain in satisfying solitary and controlled plops. 'Everyone is the same around here. Same narrow minds. The other day on my paper-round I saw this graffiti…'

Norman paused as he prepared to share his secret and reveal his fragility. Voice wavering, he felt like he was leaning back about to abseil at the Year 8 Camp. Was it time to fully expose his vulnerability and trust?

'It said "Golliwogs Out"'.

'Come on mate, you've been called worse than that.'

'You don't get it,' Norman replied indignantly, 'this wasn't a kid at school who doesn't know better. This was a stranger. I feel like I'm not wanted here, I don't fit in.'

The words came tumbling out in despair in unison with the gravel hitting the well beneath the gutter. Norman held back the tears as they welled in his eyes and betrayed his pride.

Steve wasn't sure what he could say or do. He hadn't seen his friend so angry or resigned before. It was on a different scale and made Steve uncomfortable. Part of Steve resented the attack on Blandford – he was, after all, Blandford born and bred. Something unspoken stirred between the two friends that afternoon.

CHAPTER THREE

History Lessens

In a darkened room, an image of a passive black African slave was projected beyond the illuminated tunnel of fairy dust.

'Slaves were taken from Africa and transported to America and the Caribbean.'

To accompany the humiliation, Mr Gibbons, the Humanities teacher, showed a slide of a lowly dark figure bowed down, buckling under the prowess of his plantation master, whip in hand.

Like the nicknames, this was a lesson to put Norman in his place. He was disappointed by the limitations of these 'lessons' that conspired to steal his rich identity.

As Mr Gibbons continued, Norman noticed the class bully, Chris Goodwin, smirk. A familiar reddish tinge of embarrassment and humiliation flushed through Norman. 'At least you lot don't blush,' he'd been told before. How couldn't they see the red glow in his caramel complexion? It seemed like colour blindness was selective. He felt open and raw to everyone around him, like a fresh carcass open to a pack of hyenas; as comical as a baboon's bottom.

Where was the mention of the Ashanti fighting off the British in West Africa, or the Maroon rebellion in the Caribbean? He knew there was much more to the historical narrative than this slideshow or, rather, this sideshow. Norman had seen postcards from relatives of chiefs dripping with gold, adorned in bright Kente and Adinkra symbolism. This narrative was not so black and white. His home was full of beautifully crafted masks, stools, paintings and cloth that illuminated any obfuscation of 'the dark continent'.

The rest of the lesson centred on the influence of Christian missionaries, the 'civilising mission' of Dr Livingstone and Kipling's 'white man's burden'. It reminded him of Tintin meeting the 'natives': grinning Golliwogs strangled by bowties and trussed in pinstriped trousers and Little Black Sambo. Norman wondered about the Akan sky-god Onyankopon. Did Ghanaians believe in everything they were told by Livingstone and their ilk? Did they believe in the sky deity before, during and after the Europeans came?

Norman was too shy to ask these questions out loud and draw more attention to himself. Also, experience of seeing other students boldly question Gibbons proved that this teacher did not like to stray far from his script.

'No time for that. We've got a syllabus to get through, not to mention a barrage of national tests and end of Year 10 exams,' was Mr Gibbons' stock response to critical thought. In Gibbons' high pressured and warped version of education, there was little place for inquiry and interaction. Perhaps this repeated refrain was a mantra that kept him going. The trouble was, it slowed everyone else down.

The bell signalling the end of this double period of historical humiliation could not have come quickly enough.

A true traditionalist, Gibbons made sure students sat in rows, in alternating boy/girl order. It was a tactic to quell insurrection and ensure the serfs knew their place in his futile, feudal education system. It certainly enabled him to deliver lectures to a stunned, silent audience; just the way he liked it. Gibbons presided over the rows like a Victorian factory owner. He monitored the productivity of writing copied mindlessly from the board. It was not uncommon to hear the chorus of stifled yawns from the safety of the corridor outside 10G as you passed, if you were lucky enough not to be held 'History' hostage.

The 'time in/time out' cards for toilet visits, arranged in two perfectly formed stacks on Gibbons's spartan desk, were his version of factory 'clocking-in' cards. Efficiency innovations such as this were proudly promulgated to classes by Gibbons, the overseer, at the start of each term as he eagerly continued his time and motion supervision of his charges. There was a procedure for everything in his tutorials, including dismissal. This was an opportunity for mutiny in many other classes. 'Skipper' Gibbons, on the other hand, used it as one last reminder of control for all those on board.

'Scholars, next week there is to be a test on the content of today's lesson,' was Gibbons' parting shot of adrenalin, tension and threat. 'First row, you are dismissed'. And so, row by row the students timidly filed out, partially grateful for their reprieve. Any real sense of freedom was compromised by the foreboding fear of judgement certain to follow next week.

Usually, the front row that Steve Euston sat in was dismissed first. Gibbons was a stickler for routine and had earned himself the moniker 'OCD'. This had spawned the more personal sobriquet 'OCG' (Obsessive Compulsive Gibbons or OG for short), a phrase that yielded another layer of meaning by reflecting his veteran teaching status at the school as the 'Original Gangster'. His other pseudonym was 'crater-face', owing to the pock-shaped scars that must have been the result of chronic adolescent acne in a bygone era, before facial scrubs and male manicuring became the vogue.

The severity of his countenance matched his austere persona and steely gaze. Steve normally waited for Norman after class. On this occasion though, Steve was nowhere to be seen. In fact, since their deep and meaningful chat, Norman had sensed that Steve was keeping his distance. What had Norman done to offend him?

Norman left the classroom alone in his thoughts and headed down the iron spiral staircase. He looked down through the grates. Norman's footsteps counterpointed the cacophony of Walkers crisps, a cheesy chorus of

Quavers, Mini(m)-Bites, the semi-breve of Wagon Wheels followed by rests for breath, pausing briefly before the renewed crunches of over-zealous teeth. Between the metal lattice, he saw hands hungrily cramming food into mouths from lunchboxes.

Walking across the freshly lacquered herringbone floor, Norman acclimatized to the aroma of disinfectant and semolina in the school canteen. The sickly smell of processed pizzas and oven chips wafted familiarly over him. Large aluminium water jugs wobbling at their misshapen bulbous bases sat forlornly on tables streaked with cold custard. He felt much more conspicuous on his own, entering the hubbub of clinking cutlery, crunched crisps and loud conversations punctuated by Dinner Ladies (now known as Supervisory Midday Lunch Assistants; more of a mouthful than the meals themselves) ordering students to 'behave yourselves', 'grow up' and 'learn some manners'.

It was hardly a Swiss Finishing School. Canteen pupils knew the Swiss rolls were too sickly to finish and jibed that you could catch something from the Spotted Dick. The aim here was to finish as quickly as possible, preferably without indigestion. These were the culinary dishes of South Blandfordshire, not The Ritz.

The skill was to find a free space at a table with someone he knew whilst cultivating a calm and relaxed aura. That way, he would blend in and become less of a target. Without his wingman Steve at his side, more precisely at his midriff, his mission to navigate to a safe zone was that much harder. As a student classified in the impersonal and statistically driven nomenclature of Canteen-speak, Norman was 'a packed lunch' rather than a 'hot meal'. As a result, unlike those cutting the air with their trays to ease boredom, he had less time to taxi, line up and weigh his seating options whilst queuing, waiting to be processed for his order of processed food.

The pressure was mounting. He had to decide very quickly. The row of plastic seats, suspended on metal poles, was full at the table where he caught Steve in his peripheral vision. Instead, Norman sat on the adjacent table with a collection of younger student misfits, headed by a Goth student fond of heavy mascara application, whose body language pre-empted any attempt at pleasantries or small talk. To heighten Norman's sense of rejection, he turned around and saw the full horror of Steve sitting right next to Goodwin. Immediately, Goodwin's eyes, shaded under his owl-like bushy eyebrows, held Norman's and squinted with intimidation. He was in the sights of a predator with base instincts.

'We had a great laugh fishing in the canal on Saturday, didn't we Steve?' boasted Goodwin as he held court with his audience. Norman was certain that Goodwin had raised his voice to make sure that he also heard. There was nothing Goodwin liked more than to be looked at favourably by a captive crowd of onlookers.

But why was Steve spending time with Goodwin? Norman was starting to slide further into the quagmire of vulnerability. After all, in his last proper conversation with Steve, he'd confided in him about the graffiti. The more Norman thought about it, the more he recognized now that Steve's expression that afternoon had been one of concern turned into abruptness, impatience and then even irritation or annoyance. But why was this his reaction?

Steve nodded along as Goodwin regaled his cronies with a colourful and fishy account of how they had smashed a gudgeon with a rock after landing it in their net.

'Ace, wasn't it Steve?' Goodwin beckoned his new ally to nod along in agreement for credibility. For a glorious split-second, Norman could smell his assailant's fear. He could see Goodwin's eagerness on the brink of desperation. Perhaps this corroboration helped Goodwin himself believe in the dubious events. It reminded Norman of dictators who invented national myths. The more dangerous and deranged ones brainwashed themselves.

Steve duly nodded in deference. The moment, ripe for revolution, went sour. The coup did not eventuate and Norman knew there would be a return to his state of emergency. The planets realigned and with it, Norman's place in the Universe's pecking order was restored. Goodwin liked those around him to agree, basking in his limelight. There was only room for one leading actor on this stage.

'Yeah, ace laugh.' Steve seemed a little uncertain of

himself, with his new script and status, surrounded by Goodwin and his henchmen. That was understandable, as only the week before Goodwin had referred to Steve dismissively as 'micro-dot' and seemed to have no time for him. He had literally been belittled.

Suddenly, Goodwin and Euston were side-by-side and spending time together at the weekend. It was a change in fortunes on the scale of winning the National Lottery. Each Friday night, punters would wait for the escapism, the moment when the Lottery announcer would call to 'Release the balls!' Steve's ball was off the chopping block for now; replaced by Goodwin's vice-like grip on Norman's. For Norman, it was more like a game of Russian roulette.

'OK lads, let's split,' confidently announced Goodwin. Norman bowed his head. He sensed the grim shadow of Goodwin looming above him.

'Oi Oreo. Good lesson with crater-face today, weren't it? See how useless you lot are.' Goodwin paused for effect. 'It's official, it's on the syllables!'

'Syllabus,' corrected Norman dryly. Being specific with words was a reflex that he could scarcely control despite the danger.

Undeterred by this minor blow, Goodwin prepared for the punch line, bolstered by History as well as a naïve recruit on his side. 'See…you should go back to the jungle, where you come from. Monkey. Jungle Bunny,' triumphed Goodwin. The class bully swaggered off, support crew in tow.

Feeling dazed with emptiness, Steve walked past Norman as silently as a pallbearer under the weight of his leader's expectations. Things were becoming clearer. Norman was being earmarked as the target. Goodwin was intent on proving that he was now Steve's best friend. Norman's only support was being taken away and Goodwin was revelling in his appropriation of power.

School, as well as Blandford itself, at once seemed a lonelier and more worrying place. Norman had slid unceremoniously to the bottom rung of the playground pecking order. He was at the lowest link of the food chain.

CHAPTER FOUR

DIY Role Models

Things went from bad to worse at school. After a lonely week without his friend, Norman's sense of inexorable freefall continued. The next Monday morning, Norman passed Goodwin and Steve as they were talking about their bike ride at the weekend. That made it two weeks in a row. A nail hitting harder in the coffin of humiliation. Since that conversation about the writing on the wall, Steve had not texted or called him. Not even a tweet, a Snapchat or a hastily shared message on Messenger or Instagram. It felt more like instantaneous rejection.

Whenever Norman tried to ring Steve's landline in a last-ditch attempt to make contact, he was always 'playing out with his friends', to use the parlance of Steve's mother and sister, who took it in turns to answer the phone with varying degrees of indifference. This served to underline Norman's new real life and social media status as the ditched and desperate, unfollowed and disliked ex-mate. His Facebook notifications buzzed and beeped throughout the night to remind him of the in-jokes and photos of Goodwin, Steve and the in-crowd from which he was excluded.

After their tutor group registration, Norman walked to his English class. At least Ms Evens would be interesting and take his mind off his worries for a period. She held the attention of her pupils as the youngest and most attractive member of the Brookdale staff. Ms Evens was an A-grader among D-graders. Her hair was cut in an edgy 'pixie' short crop. She wore trendy 1960s clothes to match it and donned a beret after school. Ms Evens was a beatnik symbol of university chic and poster girl revolution. She surfed the French new wave in a Breton top, black tights and an A-line pencil skirt.

Ms Evens, in terms of the Hegelian philosophy she tried to introduce, was the very antithesis of Gibbons. She liked to investigate the 'big questions' with her classes, unlike Mr Gibbons who rarely strayed from the security of the Teachers' Book and curriculum documents. She had told the class fondly of her training in 'Philosophy for Children' at university. Her classroom was an exciting world where students were welcomed as thinkers. As respected members of the community of inquiry, they were encouraged to raise their own questions about the world around them and beyond. Their role was to investigate and examine 'suggestions', couched as ideas open to scrutiny.

On that day, however, it was a worrying agenda that she facilitated. 'To develop our emotional literacy and help with our empathy training, I'd like you to consider this movie extract and think about any 'big' or philosophical questions that cannot be inferred or brainstormed. Think about anything that interests you or puzzles you. Things you agree with or disagree with. As usual, we will then harvest questions and pick out common themes for discussion.'

The theme was obvious to Norman as the drama unfolded like a pious poison-pen letter. The plot concerned an Afro-Caribbean protagonist who was called 'Omo' and 'Jungle Bunny' interchangeably. Although intended to raise awareness and debate about bullying and racism, he felt in the pit of his stomach that this would only add fuel to Goodwin's fiery tirades. The story was a cruel parallel of his own miserable plight and now it was being broadcast to the whole class, paused over and reflected upon. Norman felt alone, undone and exposed. A reality TV show gone wrong.

Norman shrank in his chair, wishing it would swallow him whole, like a bug being consumed by a Venus flytrap plant. Even a return to the milder humiliation and pain of double Eurocentric History with Gibbons was preferable to this discomfort.

Norman could hear Goodwin and his cronies, including Steve, whispering and giggling in the backbenches of the opposition. In contrast to Mr Gibbons' class, Ms Evens favoured 'fluid' or 'friendship' based groupings. As a result, Norman felt more ostracized than ever. Goodwin and his crew had sat in the back row mainly to enable them to bolt out of the door first when the lesson finished, perhaps after giving a salutatory 'dead-arm punch'. They signalled a Neanderthal goodbye by hitting the undeveloped biceps of a weaker pupil or three.

Body tensed, Norman felt a cold sweat on his furrowed brow. His heart pumped, searching for oxygen. In 'flight mode', his senses became sharper and Norman knew they were talking about him.

Anger began to rise in Norman, like a saucepan lid lifted by boiling water, combined with a simmering disappointment that he was the target yet again. Why was he always taking the heat? The rest of them took fitting in for granted. For Norman, it seemed like a far-off ambition, a moon-shot.

From that day on, Norman acquired the additional moniker 'Omo'.

'Hey Omo, how's it going?!' called out Goodwin casually across the playground as he kicked the tennis ball, its yellow-green fur stretched by aquaplaning on shallow puddles, in Norman's direction.

Soccer balls had been deemed to be too dangerous by the Risk Assessment actuaries and fun police who feared these sporting missiles. They were regarded warily as spheres of influence, calculated upon with abstracted formulae to prove that they were magnetically drawn to the many glass windows of Brookdale Upper School. Concrete and glass were the raw material of the brave new world of 1960s grand designs. Goodwin chuckled at his own joke as a cue to the bystanders to fall into line with guffawing approval. The colony naturally assented to the alpha male with awkward and nervous laughter, echoing a primeval fear that if they didn't join in, they could be the next prey.

Norman instinctively side-footed it back to Goodwin with precision.

Quickly, with a manic gaze, Goodwin switched his attention and the ball to Vikram and Chan who were innocently standing nearby. It was their turn to detonate the time bomb. 'Oi, Curry-muncher or Chink, pass us the ball back.' Vikram rolled it back cautiously. 'Thanks for the delivery service! That's what you lot do, isn't it…I'm surprised I didn't have to phone up to order it first!' smirked Goodwin, impressed that he had managed to extend a metaphor without losing the point. Chan looked over at his friend Vikram with both sympathy and empathy.

It was at this moment of ostensible weakness that Norman became aware of the inner strength of his classmates. Norman suddenly realised that Vikram and Chan had formed a bond like Steve and himself had at one time. They were part of a Sino-Indian, or Indo-Chinese pact, a bilateral and reciprocal trade agreement. Protectionism and sanctions had been issued against Goodwin's free trade in insults over the past semester.

Two layers of defence were better than one and formed a thicker skin against the jibes. Vikram and Chan had shared experiences as the children of immigrants who worked hard, literally scraping a living from the plates of the restaurant industry; one of the few multicultural businesses in Blandford. The boys were in fact ambassadors of assimilation at all costs, excluding VAT and delivery. They were part of a menu of diluted exoticisms that the community's palate could savour. Exotic without too much spice, and just a little salt and pepper to taste.

Progression had come to the point where 'tikka masala' was the Blandford Man's favourite dish to accompany lagers swilled on a Friday night 'on the town', and slurred calls for 'Paki' waiters to 'get a wriggle on' to serve alcohol-fuelled appetites. A town painted reddish-orange by pub revellers. Little did the townsfolk know that it was a spurious dish made to placate English taste buds with familiar gravy.

Meanwhile, at the 'Chinky' at the other end of Blandford, Chinese restaurants like Chan's did an oil bubbling trade in salt and vinegary fish and chips, to douse the drunken flames of nightclub goers before they entered the fantastical illusion of 'The Unicorn', Blandford's only post-midnight spot that evaded the licensing laws. Fish and chips were originally the nation's number one dish. You could read all about it as you unravelled your newspaper-wrapped meal.

Thus, Vikram and Chan were the gold and silver medallion bearers on Great Britain's oriental-ish podium. Theirs was a fine dining tradition of rebranding that had also involved the Italians. They were a living part of the syncretic legend of the Venetian merchant Marco Polo's magical travels along the Silk Route, conjuring up pasta from Chinese noodles. 'La Casa Siciliana – Italiano Ristorante' ranked bronze in Blandford's peckish 'takeaway or eat in' order.

Vikram and Chan were fellow travellers who understood each other. They both held the second-generation burden of expectation that they would escape the takeaway fate and add prestige to their families and interest to their bank balances by becoming respectable lawyers, doctors or accountants. Norman understood this pressure all too well. His mum's quest that he assimilated totally, involved her wish for his Home Counties culture and accent to enable his integration. Norman was unable to speak his mother's tongue, Twi, which he had spoken as a toddler to his maternal grandmother in Ghana before they moved to England, which caused resentment in Norman that frequently surfaced in their mother-son slanging matches.

Norman began to feel an affinity for Vikram and Chan as opposed to the mainstream that he had tried and failed to swim with. It dawned on him that they had a shared plight; fellow victims of Goodwin's myopic worldview.

As the bell rang signalling the end of lunchtime, and perhaps an era, Norman looked on in disappointment and emptiness at his former friend Steve, who returned an uncomfortable sideways glance from a distance. Nodding slowly, appreciative of a newfound solidarity with Vikram and Chan, he turned and walked towards his locker.

The days of that week passed slowly and painfully. Norman felt like he was stranded in No-Man's Land without allies. Thankfully the topics of 'Omo' and transatlantic slavery were not sustained. The curriculum was too crowded and pressurised for that. At least in Gibbons' highly structured and strict lessons, he had been assigned a table with contrived company. It offered the illusion that he was part of the school community…or any community for that matter.

It was during lesson breaks and lunchtimes that Norman struggled the most to blend in. He tried to avoid Steve and Goodwin during these unstructured times. Norman tiresomely paced the playground, pretending to walk with purpose. The faint white lines around the unnetted tennis court became his tightrope. He constantly moved around the humane shield of groups of friends and tribes that weren't his own, exhausted by trying to tag onto conversations and jokes of which he only caught the tail end. It was tough, going through the motions, rehearsing and acting out a part that wasn't really written for him, in front of an audience that frightened him. Time stood still and stuck its two fingers in his direction; two torturing hands on a watch face that he couldn't ignore.

Tuesday, Period 5, directly after a languishing lunchtime, offered brief levity. Respite took the form of Study Skills, whilst Goodwin and Euston took their Graphic Design elective. The forty minutes of bliss were 'presided' over by teacher-librarian Mr Reed, who peered nervously over his bifocals. He emphasized his preferred role as the latter part of his hyphenated job description. Books, not children, were Mr Reed's focal point.

Mr Reed was laissez-faire in his educational approach and favoured organic osmosis over the synthetic and industrial teaching techniques of Gibbons. He muttered about the demise of the Dewey system, card cataloguing and stamps. Mr Reed was thwarted by the online regimen. His sense of decimalised order was left hanging redundantly on the line. He often peered incredulously over his glasses like a bemused badger caught in the glare of car headlights.

Norman often saw Mr Reed walking home at weekends wrapped in a shabby duffel coat with a shopping trolley, exuding loneliness and bachelorhood. Mr Reed was a loner and the visiting classes interrupted his solitary bookish pursuits.

Study Skills involved students discovering the different parts of the library, classification systems and computerised loaning, all by themselves. It was a self-guided tour or inquiry approach before it became a trendy teaching technique. Mr Reed sat barricaded against generation Google, suspicious of Siri scholars inhabiting a digitally pixilated screensaver landscape, where phones were smarter than their users.

Positioned behind a stack of books at the back, he busied himself by 'accessioning' new orders, breathing on his glasses and polishing them nervously with the tatty, ribbed hem of his cardigan. As much as possible, Mr Reed avoided the responsibility of eye contact, and when pursued by a fictitious or non-fictitious request, would look at the interlocutor's left shoulder blade. It was an equally uncomfortable experience for both parties, so most students didn't even bother engaging with him. He hoped for a return to the halcyon binary days.

For most students, this 'lesson' was a chance to catch up with friends (real and virtual), scroll smartphones under desks to maintain a social media presence and extend the lunch break. It had once been the same for Norman, but now Steve had been appropriated by Goodwin. Studying now seemed an altogether more attractive and disciplined skill to pursue than the uncertain art of friendship. Books were a welcome and reliable distraction, to be opened and closed at will. Published, permanent and trustworthy in a shifting, uncertain environment.

Norman had been thinking a lot about the images of people with brown skin like his – the slaves in Gibbons's "lesson", 'Omo' and the grotesque golliwogs that he had seen as a child on marmalade jar labels when visiting his grandmother in Salisbury. These were all negative images that connected him with weakness, passivity and pity. Losers of both past and present on the wrong side of the narration formed an easy target for attacks by Goodwin and his caustic crew.

CHAPTER FIVE

Safety in Minority Numbers

Norman searched for positive black role models to redress the imbalanced scales of justice.

Sport, Norman knew through his own experience, was an arena positively charged with black achievement, adulation and even emulation. As the school Cross Country champion, middle-distance and sprint expert, Norman willingly accepted the limiting mantle but knew the unspoken rules of engagement. He was allowed momentary membership to the community via sporting success.

At the annual Sports Day, he was a 'zebra', crossing over from marginality and minority to being deemed acceptable and respectable by the majority.

Norman briefly recalled a trip with a family friend to see Leestone United play on their home artificial turf, known by locals as the 'plastic pitch', against mighty Liverpool. He again felt numbness and dread as the opposition's black players got the ball. Norman soon learnt the illogical cheers for Leestone's own black players would be met by jeers and a stream of racist abuse when the ball was passed to the 'others'. He had shrunk into his fur hooded parka that afternoon as a loud thug behind him dropped his t's for d's, elongated his vowel movements in Sarf Blan'for'sheer snarl and berated the black Liverpool players.

Richard, the family friend, had not mentioned anything about it after the match. The nervous conversation that day, especially on the awkward thirty-minute drive 'home', belied Richard's embarrassment as a lifelong Leestone fan and season ticket holder. That had been Norman's last trip to the terraces. Mind you, he'd seen worse than that on TV: bananas and sharpened fifty-pence pieces to 'make 'em pay' were hurled and accompanied by monkey chants.

Norman filled the void by romanticising about the melting pot of the Brazilian national team as the perfect passport and working visa out of the parochialism that engulfed him. His dad supported his eccentric passions fervently and had no qualms about his son failing Norman Tebbit's citizenship test whereby support of the English cricket team was a true signifier of loyalty, identity and belonging.

Norman's dad was no stranger to racial rhetoric, having witnessed first-hand Enoch Powell's inflammatory 1968 'rivers of blood' speech calling for the repatriation of immigrants and landlords' placards warning 'No Dogs, No Irish, No Blacks'. In solidarity, he had speedily arranged for a replica Brazil soccer shirt to be shipped over for his son's 14th birthday. In the gold and green of Pele, Norman felt the exoticism of being accepted and part of something bigger and bolder, a paradise where the many shades of brown were cheered on.

Now, Norman used his time in the library to begin a quest in the non-fiction sports aisle, track and field section, for positive images. '796.42 Norman, thank goodness for the Dewey system', rattled off Mr Reed proudly when asked. Soon Norman weighed up a large tome named 'An Encyclopaedia of Athletes in History'. He flicked through the pages, seeking validation, looking for a hero, a positive role model.

Momentarily, Norman was intrigued by the first random page that he opened. 'L – Liddell. Eric Henry Liddell (b.1902 d.1945), who refused to run in the heats of the 100m on a Sunday at the 1924 Olympics due to his religious beliefs, but still competed in the 400m and was victorious.' This was the sort of inspiration that Norman was looking for. He began to connect the dots and remembered Liddell now from 'Chariots of Fire'. The emotive, Vangelis-synthesized soundtrack replayed note-perfect in his mind. It was one of the few songs that Norman and his father both appreciated. The slow-motion beach scene came back to him in waves of nostalgia, causing goosebumps.

Then Norman turned to 'O' 'Owens. Jesse Owens, born James Cleveland Owens (b.1913 d.1980): the son of a sharecropper and grandson of a slave, who achieved what no other Olympian before him had accomplished. His stunning achievement of four gold medals at the 1936 Olympics in Berlin made him the best-remembered athlete in Olympic history.' Norman had just found the antidote to the daily dose of negativity. The summary piqued Norman's interest.

'Single-handedly crushing Hitler's myth of Aryan supremacy' attested the caption. The words formed a resounding death knell and epitaph on the crumbling headstone of Nazism. Above, towered Jesse Owens atop a podium among Star-Spangled Banner and swastika; symbols of relative freedom and totalitarianism.

After the Nazi seizure of power in 1933, the United States and other western democracies began to question the morality of supporting the Olympic Games hosted by Germany, a country dominated by a racist dictatorship. For African-Americans like Jesse Owens, the decision to attend the Games had an added dimension of difficulty. Already reduced to a life of a subhuman under the racially segregated policies of Jim Crow, he represented an America undergirded by the beliefs and rationalizations of white superiority.

Jesse Owens and other African American athletes, due to racial discrimination, were limited in both college and professional sports. Quick to highlight the discrimination against Jesse Owens in Berlin, little was done to address it on the home front. Owens returned 'home' to face the same invidious policies. One moment with gold aloft a dais; the next, the bottom of the rung clasping a tarnished begging bowl, facing the ignominy of racing against horses for money.

Norman read on to find how his own plight could be humbled by historic perspective, while still connected and validated. Hitler had tried to use the Olympic

Games to show the world a resurgent Nazi Germany with high hopes that German athletes would dominate and be victorious. Nazi propaganda promoted concepts of Aryan racial superiority and depicted ethnic Africans as inferior. Owens countered this by winning four gold medals right under their haughty noses, in the galvanising glare of the propaganda machine.

Norman could not help to see their parallel plights against ignorance now crossing over and intertwining. Goodwin's bombastic propaganda should also be undermined and silenced by positive achievement. Reading Owens' struggle now placed his problems within a sharper focus.

Buoyed by this moral victory, Norman continued his crusade to a familiar haunt; the African History 'section' of the library, Norman's preferred libation at the barcodes. He frequented this area of the library in a search to affirm a more rounded History than that offered by Gibbons. Norman though soon realised that his dad had more African History books in his study.

Norman imbibed the sour cocktail of perennial disappointment mixed with no surprise. Kept soberly in place, he compared the half a dozen texts, intimidated by the other histories shelved in dusty cabinets proportionate to their degree of world dominance. Europe commanded four shelves, the Americas three and Asia one in descending order of Eurocentric historiography. Norman ignored this sliding scale of world power. The book that intrigued him most was 'The Book of African Names and Proverbs' by

Professor Afua Osei. He instantly recognised the name as Ghanaian. The rest of the books were clearly written about Africa by those without African names.

He was struck by the Yoruba phrases. His father had first taught in Nigeria before moving to Ghana and had told Norman about the complex naming systems. Norman's Ghanaian, to be more precise, Akan day name was Kwabena, Twi for Tuesday born. It was a source of pride, connecting him with his diasporic cousins of past and present: Kwasis, Kwadjos, Kwame Nkrumahs and Kofi Annans. It was unapologetically Ghanaian and proud. It was a potent symbol that conjured images of an imagined Ghanaian homeland where the grass was greener, the bananas turned to plantain and the blight of potatoes to yummy yams. Where life was sweeter and more exotic than Blandford's overcast skies, graffitied walls and glass ceilings.

His only regret was that it was not his first name which could be worn like a badge. Some Nigerian tribes, he had been told, often had whole phrases and sentences, mini-narratives to describe them. West African naming systems were more alive and vital than Blandford's Kevins, Karens and Waynes. In a ritual of self-actualisation, Norman looked up his name Kwabena. The following chapter 'Nigerian Naming Systems – Yoruba' had a profoundly erudite-sounding italicised subtitle '*ile ni a n wo, ki a to so omo l'oruko*' and bold translation: **one pays attention to the family before naming a child**'. Norman began to enunciate the empowering magical mantra in his head until he came to the word 'omo'. The word OMO was Yoruba and not just a detergent used as an ethnic cleansing agent to wash Goodwin's dirty laundry of thoughts in public.

Driven to discover more, light-headed with relief and book in hand, Norman gripped the faded grey-crossed base of a tatty swivel chair spewing its foam cushioning from within. Curling his toes in anticipation, Norman positioned himself at a free computer. He searched an online English-Yoruba dictionary. 'Omo' meant child. Norman found in this a curious consolation; his father had taught him at an early age to be aware of the many meanings, contexts and nuances of words. Norman remembered his dad's academic pun, encouraging him to 'graze in the semantic fields'. Each time Goodwin called him 'Omo' he would remember that he was a child of Africa.

Norman reflected on how this creative appropriation was part of a lineage, featuring rappers before him. He had scoured their bio's courtesy of 'Hip Hop Connections' and frequently engaged in further reading on Rap website Wikipedia. Pride swelled inside him as he read how they had taken ownership of the 'N-word', casting off the shackles of oppression and rendering their opponents speechless in one semantic bi-syllabic move.

CHAPTER SIX

Norman Has a Dream

The following Tuesday during Study Skills in Period 5, Norman borrowed a biography of Jesse Owens and 'A Short History of the US Civil Rights Struggle' that he found in the Americas section.

Norman read voraciously about the racial discrimination and segregation faced by African Americans in the 1960s. He learned about nonviolent protests, civil disobedience, crises and dialogue between activists and the government. Wondering wide-eyed at the power of mass action (bus boycotts, 'freedom rides', sit-ins and marches), Norman found inspiration in the passing of the Civil Rights Act of 1964.

He worried less about Goodwin and Steve, preferring to befriend uplifting historical figures such as Martin Luther King, Rosa Parks and Malcolm X. Their eloquent appeals to Christian brotherhood, US idealism, refusal to make room for a white bus passenger and courageous advocacy, made for a heady mixture.

Upon sober reflection, Blandford and indeed Blandfordshire was more progressive than Alabama in the 1960s. The struggle, though, was not over. The racism that Norman experienced was subtler but nonetheless present.

'I have a dream that one day, down in Alabama, with its vicious racists …one day right there in Alabama, little black boys and black girls will be able to join hands with little white boys and white girls as sisters and brothers.'

Norman breathed it in as if summoning ancestral spirits.

Buffering.

'I have a dream that my four little children will one day live in a nation where they will not be judged by the colour of their skin, but by the content of their character. I have a dream today.'

Norman reflected on how, almost half a century later, he was still being judged by some for the wrong reasons.

Rewind.

'And when this happens, and when we allow freedom to ring, when we let it ring from every village and every hamlet, from every state and every city, we will be able to speed up that day when all God's children, black men and white men, Jews and Gentiles, Protestants and Catholics, will be able to join hands and sing in the words of the old Negro spiritual:

Free at last! Free at last! Thank God Almighty, we are

free at last!'

Norman viewed Martin Luther King's 'I Have a Dream' speech over and over again. It felt like he was being spoken to directly. Blandford needed to let this message ring in the ears of the bigots, the disenfranchised and the indifferent. It would be up to Norman to speed up that day in Blandford. But he was unsure how. Now more than ever, he felt close to the other minority groups of Blandford and despised the casual racism flippantly levelled against them.

Basking in the rhythm and rhetorical elegance of a shared utopian dream, Norman jumped at the gentle tapping on his half-open bedroom door.

'The repetition of a phrase at the beginning of sentences. I believe it is repeated eight times, as Martin Luther King paints a rich picture of an integrated and unified America for his audience. Very powerful use of language Norman.'

His father had overheard the speech on his way along the hallway. He travelled through the artery of the house, resplendent with framed Adinkra symbols, initially routed to make a strong instant coffee as a pick-me-up from the floor stacked high with A-level exam marking that awaited him. He became animated.

'The speech alludes to Psalm 30:5, Isaiah 40:4-5 *"I have a dream that every valley shall be exalted,"* and Amos 5:24 *"But let justice roll down like water"*. Furthermore, King alludes to the opening lines of

Shakespeare's Richard III: *"Now is the winter of our discontent...made glorious summer..."* when he remarks that *"this swelling summer of the Negro's discontent will not pass until there is an invigorating autumn".'*

His voice, taking flight in its own dream, continued.

'The speech uses rhetorical lenses such as voice merging, of his and his religious predecessors, prophetic voice through the use of persuasive words to speak for the population, and dynamic spectacle. To quote Aristotle, *"a weak hybrid form of drama"* – pure theatre.'

There was so much to learn, thought Norman.

'How do you know all this dad?'

'Like you, I was interested, I am interested. The more I found out, the more I wanted to know...and I'm still finding out. One key is turned to open a door, you turn a corner and another confronts you. It is never-ending.' Perhaps this was the lifelong learning about which his abstruse casual teacher, Mr Neal, would often preach. Norman wanted to impart wisdom with metaphors like this one day.

'I recommend you look up a chap called W.E.B. du Bois who, among others, inspired King. Although born in the United States, he died in Ghana, your birthplace. His cause included people of colour everywhere in their struggles against colonialism and imperialism. We stand on the shoulders of giants, Norman.'

He had grown to love his father's recommendations, as they often led his mind to new and interesting destinations.

Just as Martin Luther King had stood on W.E.B. du Bois's shoulders, Norman wanted to stand on the shoulders of his dad and the members of the US Civil Rights movement.

A great source of pride for Norman, yet humility for his father, Norman's dad had studied at Cambridge University and was a fellow of Trinity College. It was there that he had, to use his father's antiquated parlance, 'read English Literature, followed by Theology at Westcott House'. At one time he was intrigued by a school of Christian atheism: this thought always made Norman's head spin; he was a free thinker. Before a planned return to the more conventional fold to embark on a life in the priesthood, his dad's love of literature and curiosity took him to a teaching position in West Africa. It was there that he met Norman's mum and the rest, as they say, is History...as well as English and Theology.

Cambridge had been a passport from working-class Wiltshire for his father. He grew up in a Victorian terrace just beyond the medieval walls of the cathedral city Salisbury, but this had not stopped him from entering that other world. His grandfather was a railway porter and his grandmother a secretary at the local auctioneer. The mortgage for the house was in fact a generous loan from the auctioneer William Wallis to the tune of £3,500 at the time, a tidy sum. Academic pursuits were not valued in the household. Much to Norman's grandfather's disappointment, his father showed little interest in the tool shed, preferring the company of books to lathes, reading late into the night with a torch under the bedcovers. When his plot was uncovered, his parents would tell him 'You'll go blind if you don't give those blasted books a break, the bed is a place for you to rest'.

As a young child, Norman's father had displayed a peculiarly precocious interest in the architecture of the local medieval cathedral and the Saxon churches of surrounding villages. He would go on long bike rides along country lanes to visit, sketch and research them. He developed a passion for Early Church Music and snuck into Matins at the cathedral, a stroll from his home.

Norman's father was the first of the family to pass his 12 Plus exam and began studying at Bishop Wordsworth's Grammar school in the Cathedral Close. During the annual family holiday to visit his grandmother, he would have a glint in his eye and a wry smile on his face each time father and son passed by the Salisbury Civic Society's blue plaque on the ivy-eroded red brick. It boasted 'WILLIAM GOLDING, Novelist & Nobel Prize Winner, was a schoolmaster here 1945-1962'. Golding had told Norman's father that he would never make it to University to read English.

The concept of 'standing on the shoulders of giants'

was less abstract for his father. Isaac Newton, also a Trinity fellow, wrote in a 1676 letter, 'If I have seen further it is by standing on the shoulders of giants.' These words were inscribed underneath Newton's pensive statue, apple about to fall upon head, next to a willow-curtained River Cam.

Norman's father had once informed him that the metaphor of dwarfs standing on the shoulders of giants came from Latin. Originally derived from Greek mythology, the blond giant Orion carried a servant on his shoulders *'nanos gigantum humeris insidentes'* and expresses the meaning of *'discovering truth by building on previous discoveries'*. In the 12th-century, modern scholars looked to Ancient Greece and Rome for inspiration.

John of Salisbury was one such scholar. In his 1159 book 'Metalogicon', which refined and adapted this classical work, he wrote, 'We are like dwarfs sitting on the shoulders of giants. We see more, and things that are more distant than they did, not because our sight is superior or because we are taller than they, but because they raise us up, and by their great stature add to ours.' The coincidence of a theologian from his home cathedral city had piqued the interest of Norman's father at the time. Like so many seemingly obscure facts, his father had woven them together for Norman as a rich tapestry of trivia on one of their trips to the university town.

Norman pondered if these disparate tales were coincidences or part of a grand plan. Was he part of

Martin Luther King's plan? Norman suddenly had an image of Jesse Owens passing the metaphorical baton of equality in a race against time and ignorance.

CHAPTER SEVEN

Pan Africanism

Pan-Africanism encouraged the solidarity of Africans worldwide to 'unify and uplift people' of shared descent. It was time that Brookdale's minorities were similarly unified and uplifted. With this new knowledge, Norman saw with fresh eyes and heard with disgust the casual racism that was part of everyday playground speech against the 'Chinks', 'Pakis' and 'Spics'. Most students, like himself, Vikram and Chan, turned the other cheek and tactically ignored the slights and humiliation.

There was always, however, an exception to every rule, and at Brookdale Upper it came in the burly and five o'clock-shadowed form of Michael Carozza. Even his name exuded a hybrid confidence. He was larger than life in 3D widescreen, waltzing nonchalantly to a 'Godfather-like' soundtrack of accordion, mandolin and doleful trumpet to announce his ever-dramatic entry to the South Blandfordshire scenery.

Carozza, known endearingly by the Anglicized appellation 'Crozzy', was the apple of everyone's eye, even though he was an 'I-Tie'. The youngest son of Sicilian parents, he was born in Blandford but proudly talked about 'going home to Vespas, girls, beaches and a plumbing apprenticeship at sixteen'; probably in that order. His exercise books were emblazoned with a row of medals to attest his status: the green, white and red Bandiera Italia AGV motorcycle stickers were stuck alongside the unapologetic black and white stripes of Juventus, '*Forza Juve!*' Crozzy spoke effortlessly in a cheeky, mellifluous blend of Bob Hoskins South Blandfordshire brogue and Sicilian sing-song cadence. The girls loved him; the boys even more.

Norman began to marvel at how Michael, unlike the rest of the second-generation Anglo-Italians, attracted respect and street credibility at grassroots, school soccer pitch and tarmac playground level.

Brookdale's most sizeable minority, if that wasn't a contradiction in terms, was its Italian population. After the Second World War, Blandford's Marley Vale Brick & Tile Company found itself short of labour for the post-war reconstruction boom. So, between 1951 and the early 1960s, it recruited more than 7,500 men from the villages of southern Italy.

Each man was given a medical examination, a ticket to England and a bed, often in a converted prisoner of war camp. With loneliness, cold weather and terrible food the only distractions from their heavy work, most men did not see out their four-year contracts. But some did. They bought houses in South and Mid-Blandfordshire and paid their families' passage to come and join them later, in the 1960s. As a result, by the 1970s and 1980s, reunited families began raising children who knew less about 'home' in southern Italy. Plans of returning faded and they had been rudely awoken from the immigrant dream. One such family were the Carozzas, but again

Michael was an exception in his continued fervour for the Old Country.

To bolster Norman's fragile sense of community and search for solidarity, he had become obsessed with the parallels between the Italian community, the Windrush generation and his family's more solitary and unusual migration. On a grander scale, between the arrival of the Empire Windrush passenger ship in 1948 and 1970, nearly half a million immigrants from the Caribbean came to Britain which, in 1948, faced severe post-war labour shortages.

The nearest this community had come to Norman was at Leestone. It was tantalisingly close at 14 miles from his hometown yet another world away as the train line connecting the towns had been abandoned in the 1960s as part of council cost-cutting measures. These cuts continued in the present day and were now known by local politicians and councillors in Orwellian doublespeak as 'austerity measures, streamlined or multimodal services'; their rationalism was irrational.

Leestone was only marginally quicker to reach than a less-than-affordable off-peak train ride to London. The surviving bus line was slow and unreliable. Aside from the shopping excursions of yesteryear, Norman hadn't been there for years.

As he got older, however, Norman became a regular on the bus to Leestone, initially using it as a vehicle for his quest for the perfect "retro with a modern twist" afro-dread flat-top with fade. There were no Afro-Caribbean hairdressers in Blandford and he was growing tired of his traumatic visits to the traditional barber 'H. Watling' just across the canal bridge. The bridge connected Blandford with its hyphenated neighbouring town of Buzzard. It was thought the name 'Buzzard' came from Theobald de Busar who was Prebendary of the Dean of Lincoln as it was within that diocese at the time.

The grandiose Blandford-Buzzard was shortened to Blandford by most of its more down-to-earth residents. Besides, new housing estates were built on the more level and less boggy land of Blandford, so it had a far bigger population.

'H. WATLING' was written in minimalist Scrabble tile lettering and offered a glimpse of the short back and sideshows on special offer. Harold had a reputation for enjoying a whisky-fuelled lunch and unfortunately the only time Norman could visit him was after school on weekdays, due to weekend sporting commitments.

He stoically awaited his fate under the scissors and clippers, as he half-listened to pensioners and a slightly younger Watling wax lyrically about caravan holidays. A native to Yorkshire, Watling was the only one present who emphasized the last syllable (of each word) as they extolled the virtues of the golden days of Brylcreem and the "DA" (the irreverently named "duck's arse" cuts). Norman had that familiar sinking feeling as he sat back in one of the heavily padded burgundy barber chairs, awaiting another humiliation, as Harold ignored his requests and proceeded headlong, or rather hair-long, towards his own interpretation of what needed to be done to tame his wiry afro.

As usual, Norman left the salon only £5.50 lighter but in a mood that was somewhat heavier and wearing a beanie to disguise his outwardly misshapen hair disappointment. It was a familiar routine. He would go home, shampoo his hair and tease out the imperfections of the disjuncture between the golden wiry afro that sat wonkily atop the clipped number one sides. It looked like an uneven home-baked loaf of bread that had risen with more yeast on one side. Only time healed the follicle divide.

Thus, Norman had vowed to visit an authentic Afro-Caribbean barber in Leestone at the next available opportunity. Two months passed by and with it the wiry afro had regrouped to Jackson Five proportions. Norman had researched barbers in an exhausting Internet and Yellow Pages trawl of Afro-Caribbean sounding names. It was 'Def Row Cutting Corner' on Anglia Road, near the disused train line that enticed him by name alone. When booking the appointment by phone, the bombastic aplomb of 'Def Row', enunciated in Jamaican patois, confirmed his choice.

Hair had increasingly become a signifier for Norman. Just as the Black Panthers proudly rocked Afros or Rastas shook their locks, carefully cultivated hairdos connected Norman to the diaspora and motherland. He wanted to be judged by and rooted in it, particularly as he had endured a strained relationship with his hair since toddlerhood.

Norman's hair drew the wrong sort of attention and was often touched without invitation or reference to coil pattern.

'You're hurting my hair,' he cried as a three-year-old, as his mum brushed the complaints aside in a quest for the perfectly spherical 1970s afro.

In Lower School, 'nitty Nora the hair explorer' (the outreach local health nurse) disrupted the sphere with her own ignorance. He hated his hair being touched. The invasive palms of her hands parting his bushy afro before delving deeper and penetrating it with her fingertips, pink fleshy metal detectors awaiting treasured hair lice. Yet it was the cause of so much attention.

In the early part of Middle School, hairstyles relaxed in a throwback to the mid-1980s, U.S inspired 'soul glow'. Not living near any Afro-Caribbean hair shops became a catalyst for his creativity. Norman bravely attempted using 'apple peach hair gel' from the pharmacy chain store Superdrug. His hair began to glow before quickly drying out before his eyes, hardening fast with a build-up of white flakes. He learned to wait for the rain to give his hair a 'glo' until the next shampoo, when the wiry 'fro' would re-emerge.

More recent sporadic attempts at rope twists or dreadlocks unravelled in the wash. Desperate efforts to bind his locks with egg whites built up his frustration.

He'd even read that fabric softener might help, but this ended in an irritated scalp and burning forehead. His only hair counsellors were (h)air-brushed rappers and musicians plastered on his bedroom walls, sporting the finished product.

This to-ing and afro-ing of styles and harrowing hair trials left their mark on Norman's scalp and for years he had resigned himself to his mum's utilitarian, short afro cuts. Executed with scissors but without the 'buzz' of clippers, his hair sprang back defiantly in days.

Indeed, it had been his desire for clippers that had mistakenly led him up Watling's suburban garden path.

He was nervously excited on the day of departure. The X15 South Blandfordshire bus wheezed and sighed in its own exhausted fumes, stopping at surrounding villages to let handkerchief-head adorned Old Aged Pensioners fumbling for coins or season passes to alight. Norman prepared himself for discomfort that might await him of a different sort to the usual 'H. Watling' visits. He knew that his middle-class English accent and unworldly and un-streetwise Blandford ways would betray him. He had conducted anthropological research on what to expect via the only Afro-Caribbean barbershop sitcom 'Desmonds'. The show was set in Peckham Rye. Clearly, the barbershop was a community hub and social scene. He longed to join the fictional disparate diaspora of Guyanese Desmond, his old friend Porkpie and Gambian student

Matthew.

Gradually, the Middle English villages became connected by condensed housing schemes as they joined the concrete sprawl and satellite suburbs of Dunstone and Hillnock Regis. Detached homes blurred into semi-detached and terraced rows as the unfamiliar sight of more brown faces appeared on the bus. Blandford accents became suffused with English from the Indian subcontinent, African and Caribbean creoles, Cockney and its recent offshoot, Multicultural London English. Fried and jerk chicken shops, African restaurants and saris on mannequins commingled with Poundland and Ladbroke betting shops. Gone were the Conservative Clubs and Country Women's Associations of Blandford, replaced with a large 'Welcome to the Borough of Leestone – home to millinery and car manufacturing' sign.

Norman had undertaken preparatory online research in Study Skills for that maiden voyage and had learned that Leestone was situated on the River Lee. With nearing 180,000 residents, it was one of England's most populous towns without official city status. With London and Birmingham alongside it, Leestone was a slightly less attractive cultural mecca for Norman's transformation of Dick Whittington's search for multicultural riches. The legend of the ascent of a poor orphan from rags to riches. Leestone was located 30 miles from London and 14 miles from Blandford. Norman unearthed, from digging into Encyclopaedia Britannica online, an early settlement dating back 2,500 years but the town had its foundation in the 6th-century as a Saxon outpost. The main attraction was the country house, Leestone Hoo. Apparently, 'Hoo' meant spur of the hill. Anyhoo, it was its more recent history that galvanised Norman's imagination.

The town (not quite city) was famous for hat-making and the large Pimlico Motors Factory. It dawned on Norman that this was why Leestone United, winners of the Football League Cup in 1988, was known as the 'Hatters'. Of more interest though, was the Leestone International Carnival, held before the last Monday in May and the largest one-day carnival of its kind in Europe. It also boasted the largest Saint Patrick's Day Festival this side of Boston. Of greatest kudos to Norman, however, was the last sentence of the website: 'the large Irish community in Leestone, together with the large Pakistani and West Indian communities, attracted by the allure of employment at the Pimlico car plant.' The dream triumvirate of Irish, Asian and Black.

Often mistaken as a 'Paki', Norman felt invested in that community. As the largest and nearest ethnically visible 'other population' to Blandford, the Pakistani community were singled out for special treatment. Ironically, of course, many hard-working Pakistani families travelled to Blandford, setting up corner stores, thereby resuscitating the ailing local economy. Sadly, these contributions were overlooked and usurped by the far-right chant of 'Pakis outnumbered ten to one'. It was one of Brookdale's favourite playground refrains.

Anglia Road, home to 'Def Row', was the stop before the ugly concrete Civic Centre; a flamboyant shopping mecca complete with gaudy pink plastic flamingos, their wrinkled claws submerged in a neon-lit jacuzzi of bronze and silver coins. Perhaps locals tossed money in there wishing to escape the boarded precincts and dying car industry of the town. Norman remembered his safaris there as a young child in a brightly lit and distant past; the sweet smell of plantain, the rough hides of yam next to the bakery selling iced buns.

He left the bus after hesitantly waiting for the driver to signal that this was his stop. He'd arranged to be told this at the start of the journey in Blandford before he was embarrassed by the pressure to appear streetwise. Next time, Norman coached himself, he would press the bell with confidence and assume the air of a local. He walked over the anti-slip felt-grey bridge that resembled a giant, occasionally sparkled nail file. It connected light industrial units to a dishevelled parade of shops, most of which winked at him knowingly with their warning signs of corrugated iron and plywood boarded-up self-defence. Locals, he would discover later, called it 'Tin Town'.

After the Second World War, there was a severe shortage of accommodation known as 'London overspills', and new building materials were employed to save both time and money. The majority were British Iron and Steel Federation Houses, which used sheet metal (tin) for the upper parts of the construction.

Half a century later, most of these houses were still standing in Norman's view, although he could see the 'revamping by cladding' artifice used by the local council and private owners to disguise the original metal. Soon, only a few of these properties would show the original painted metal. Phone boxes with smashed windows and graffitied bus stops littered the streets, reminding him of one of Mr Neal's lessons about Kristallnacht.

A glance at his phone confirmed that the barbershop was nearby. In fact, it was the only shop open for business on the truncated parade. In his heightened state of anxiety, Norman recalled sketchy memories of the shop itself. With a mixture of relief and dismay, he went through the slats of plastic-ribboned doorway to discover that he was the only customer. A middle-aged lady, younger than his mum, with neatly cultivated corn-rows and only sprouts of grey hair showing, greeted him. In a light and playful Jamaican lilt, she asked 'What gwaan?' and upon appraisal of her client added generously, 'What can I do for you darling? It's only me 'ere today. Me cousin' Marvin, the other stylis', is a lickle poorly today.'

Norman described his intended cut in a self-conscious and self-effacing tone amid shy stuttering. He was accustomed to the nervousness of his nerdish ways.

'Well, anyways, I'm Precious, pleased to meet you, and what's your name?'

'It's, erm, Norman. Umm…err…I was thinking abou' an afro-dread flat top with fade…' He paused, realising it sounded like something you might order from Mr Whippy. Norman had attempted to drop his t's to affect what he considered to be a more street-smart, working-class tone in tune with his surroundings, but this only served to make him more awkward. This was like du Bois's 'double-consciousness', the internal conflict involved in perennially looking at yourself through the prejudices, pity and contempt of white racist society, in reverse.

Her retro Flo-Jo-esque nails, inspired by the glitzy late 1980s American track and field athlete, adorned in stars and stripes, buried into Norman's hair. 'How I'd love 'air like dis. Is' got a fine texture…' Her words elided like a soothing lullaby to balm Norman's nerves.

'This is wha' I was thinking of…'

He released his saved images and scrolled through his phone like a lifeline connecting his hairstyle dreams to the reality of a Leestone salon.

'A'it. I can do that fi you, na problem.'

Norman sat back in relief as she faded the sides with sharp-angled repeated up-thrusts, trimmed and loosely twisted the top, just as he did after visits to Watling.

'Mmm…it's a bit lopsided but we'll straighten it out,' she chuckled, sucking her teeth softly and nodding reassuringly.

'I hope you don't straighten it too much,' quipped Norman 'I'm proud of my curls!'

The vulnerability of putting his hair in her hands encouraged a new openness in Norman. He offered an abridged life story, confessed his unusual upbringing and even that he lived in Blandford. He again unashamedly pronounced his t's. Norman was surprised to learn that Precious had looked at houses in the Blandford area and wanted to move to a quieter and safer neighbourhood. It appeared that the grass was always greener, on both sides of the urban/ suburban fence.

Norman left the salon with an unfamiliar spring in his step, looking at the few intact glass windows in the shops as confirmation of how pleased he was with his new look. The cracks in the glass gave way to the less distorted image that he'd hoped for. He was content to wait the hour and fifteen minutes for the returning X15 bus. Norman plugged in his earphones and smoothed his expertly faded sides in the motion of a 50-metre backstroke swimmer, keenly verifying that he was not dreaming. Then Norman relaxed into the politically conscious and fitting beats of Giddy Vandal.

In the wintry haze of mid-afternoon on his Saturday adventure, the X15 meandered back through the quilted patchwork of country lanes, past the Garden Centre and the geometric roofscape of the low-rise 'Meadowlane' council estate. In a cruel twist of urban planning fate, Meadowlane had become famous for its concrete cow sculptures. A cruel joke from the university-educated upon the working classes who had to live amid bucolic euphemisms in concreted jungles. As the bus passed the lower-middle-class Brookdale estate, Norman's thoughts switched back to Brookdale's Italian connection.

The modest and affordable neighbourhood, which his school largely served, was popular among those with Italian heritage. Norman looked on appreciatively at the ornate gardens; faux Corinthian PVU columns keeping the 1970s-built semi-detached houses grounded, and elaborate laced net curtains tied together in flourishing bows. It was not unusual to see older, first-generation Italian widows dressed veil to toe in black, peering out of those pristine white laced curtains. The area flourished with Italian cafes and delicatessens, with arrays of cured and smoked meats hanging like stalactites from the ceilings of Aladdin's cave. Upon entering, Italian was the sole language of transaction by customers in the piquant air of ripe peppers, sausage and pickled artichokes. Norman couldn't wait to get back to school to see Michael Carozza again, eager to cement the bricks of his recent interests in 'Little Italy'.

CHAPTER EIGHT

Norman History

The next Monday, Norman rushed to his first-period French class early and sat near Michael 'Crozzy'. For most of Brookdale Upper, speaking in a foreign tongue was a rude awakening to the week, evidenced by the fact that it was the lowest attended elective in Year 10. At the start of the year, the measly class of fifteen linguists had been told that, with any fewer students, the course was in jeopardy of being cut. It was Mr Line's thinly veiled warning; study the weekly vocabulary lists and verb tenses or jeopardise everyone's fortunes en français. Over half of the attendees were Italian, opting for a course of language study close to their home tongue. Italian, though, was only a subject choice offered informally at the Saturday schools in the nearby Brookdale Community Hall.

'La banlieue,' whispered Norman, within Crozzy's earshot, keen to help his friend.

'La banlieue,' stated Michael calmly, stretching out the syllables mellifluously, with the bluff of an A-list celebrity.

'Bien Michel. Exactement mon eleve. That is the correct term for suburbs en francaise. Tres bien.' Norman could hear the Franglish praise but could not make out any lip movements under Mr Line's walrus-like moustache. His hirsute handlebars almost joined his stubbly mandible but not quite enough to form a beard. Above, lay a duck's slightly upturned sizeable beak and permanently knitted critical brows.

Norman had rescued Michael and the class from a lecture on falling educational standards, and how once upon a time, classes were immersed in the whole language model. It was a distant and misty utopia where any utterance of English was outlawed by the authorities, aka Her Majesty's Inspectorate of Schools, known in the trade interchangeably as HMI or MI6. The new arrangements seemed to suit Monsieur Line though, as he would often go 'off-piste' from his lesson plan to patronise the students in English.

He did this with relish on the auspicious occasion of their inaugural French lesson, which served to all intents and purposes as a naming ceremony. He had spent the first fifteen minutes telling a boy called Salvatore how his name meant saviour, a fact that his parents presumably knew and passed onto him. Monsieur Line continued his Romantic dissection of the name, explaining how it was spelt Salvador 'en espagnol' but in his class he would be known as 'Salvateur', naturalement. Stephen Brumble, who sat next to Norman, found his name truncated to the glamorous Etienne.

Norman felt slightly aggrieved when Line explained that Norman would simply have to change the pronunciation of his name to, "NOR-mahn', even though the Old German origin of it means "northerner".

It was used in England even before the Norman Conquest and may have referred to people from Norway or some other region north of Britain.' Line sneered as he explicated in his nasal drawl and pensively popped a Polo mint in his mouth to fortify himself.

'Sir, I thought this was French, not Medieval History!' quipped the class clown Alan Rudzinski. This met with further furrowing causing a monobrow.

Line continued unperturbed, as ever ignoring his hecklers.

'But it's very appropriate as the group of people who conquered England in 1066 were called Normans and originated in Scandinavia. They stopped for about a century to conquer and settle northern France, the region known as Normandie,' emphasising his point with the demonstrative upturned palm of a mime artist, 'before moving across the English Channel to attack Britain from the south. You're in good company. And the rest is history NOR-mahn, or should I say Norman History! No doubt Mr Gibbons has taught you that already.' Line recalled a wealth of historical facts about northern Europe with ease. He dared to diverge and see links as only an expert did; unlike Gibbons's potted histories.

Line was one of a string of eccentric members of staff. During the summer holidays, he drove coaches to the Continent to earn additional funds to satisfy his penchant for Polo mints and cigarettes. Presumably, this was where he honed his gruff, authentic French accent. His forty-a-day smoking habit added to the ambience, part and parcel of the driving trade, scarcely masked by an equally impressive mint intake.

Norman's French teacher, preferably addressed as professeur, did not shy away from preaching to the students about his 'philosophie' – namely that he could understand neither TV nor football. "Professeur" Line prided himself in being alternative, a self-proclaimed Marxist, Classicist and Luddite. He offered provocation to mainstream scorn. He lived for it.

'It's just a group of men chasing around an inflatable ball of leather.'

On one occasion, Line had explained how football and cricket pitches had been much larger in a mawkish bucolic past but industrialisation had enclosed freedom and leisure, seen in the reduced boundaries in both work and play. Norman had been fascinated by the literal and symbolic contraction of lifestyle. Line rejoiced in his rejection of popular culture and it made him seem more foreign to his pupils, even though he originally hailed from Leestone. That was the intention no doubt. Thus Line curated and projected an image as an intrepid agent provocateur of the status quo; aged enfant terrible of the education establishment.

'Thanks for that one pal,' chuckled Michael at the end of the lesson, slapping Norman heartily on the back. 'You'd've thought that with Italy being so close to France I'd be better armed…well as Line often says they can be "faux amis"…'

'Do you speak Italian then Crozzy?' quizzed Norman, keen to find out more about his heritage. As a convert to Pan-Africanism and a newly enlightened torchbearer for Pan-Blandfordism, it was important to know these things. Knowledge was powerful and a union of nations was even more so.

'Nah mate, I understand it but can't speak it.'

This reminded Norman of his long-lost Ghanaian cousins in London who responded to his Uncle Maxwell and Aunty Viv's demands in English, a symbol of the Black British identity and adolescent rebellion. This linguistic connection encouraged Norman to see the similarities. Pan-Blandfordism was a force to be recognised.

'Same for my cousins who understand Twi, one the languages in Ghana, where…I was born…wh-where my mum comes from.' Norman eagerly tripped over his words and regained his footing on their newly found shared terrain.

He'd never talked to Steve about this kind of thing.

Over the next few days, Norman and Michael talked more during and after lessons. Norman had been desperate to know but he was embarrassed to ask how Michael kept Goodwin and co at bay.

As the weeks passed, the initial novelty of Michael asking, 'You going my way? Bramble Close?' had become an end of the school day tradition. That afternoon, as Norman made his way to the school gates, he could see Michael standing his ground in a heated exchange, shielding two younger students from Goodwin. Apart from Michael, the others shoe-gazed uncomfortably, shifting their scuffed shoes like a trio of naughty schoolboys, which of course they were. Michael wore an uncharacteristically stern expression and pointed at Goodwin's chest.

Norman slowed his advance and waited for their departure.

'What was all that about?' he asked.

'I can't hack bullies. That lowlife was giving it the 'I-Ties' routine to my cousins. You'd've thought he'd got the message by now,' he sighed. Sweat was forming on Michael's brow and he wiped it with his Juventus sweatband. Norman noticed Michael had started sweating profusely when he'd been asked the question about 'la banlieue' the other week.

'That lowlife only goes for easy targets. He still tries it on with me when his gang are around him but on his own he's nothing.'

Michael's method of direct action against his tormentor mesmerised Norman. It reminded him of Malcolm X's advocation of armed self-defence that stood in contrast to Martin Luther King's brand of non-violent action.

'Anyway, let's forget about that loser.'

Norman was about to tell Michael about his own run-ins with Goodwin but didn't want to upset his new friend any further. The last time he'd confided in an ally, things had not gone so well. Norman didn't want bitter history to repeat itself. He didn't want pity. Norman wanted a friend who liked him for what he was, not for what he wasn't. It was a conversation that could wait.

So far, with his new alliance with Michael, he had forgotten about Steve and Goodwin. They had kept more of a distance. With Crozzy at his side, Norman was a harder target and less entertaining prospect for Goodwin. Things were calm; for now.

CHAPTER NINE

Suspended Belief

'Come on lads. Blandford versus the Rest of the World. How'z about it?"

Goodwin, soccer ball on hip, had found his courage now that his choreographed cronies, including Euston, circled like vultures around him.

'Get some of yer foreign legion and we'll give you a match,' challenged Goodwin to Norman and Michael. 'Look, Hemsway is on duty, there'll be no funny business, promise. Scouts honour,' leered Goodwin with a phoney salute.

Norman recalled a sobering anecdote his father had relayed to him about Baden-Powell founding the scouting movement of which his father had been a nostalgic member. His famous book, 'Scouting for Boys' was its Bible. The book went on to be the most successful post-war English-language publication after the Bible. Blind childish faith in the Scout movement had been replaced with disbelief when Norman's father stumbled across the sinister truths behind this quintessentially British historical figure.

Having taught in Ghana and visited Kumasi's Cultural Centre, Norman's father had learnt that the same

Baden-Powell was a British army major who had, in 1895, led the colonial war on the capital of the Ghanaian kingdom, the Ashanti Empire. His ideology was shaped by the vanquishing and theft of the Ashanti's cultural heritage. Baden Powell's military experiences strengthened his feelings of white colonial superiority over Africans.

Despite his writing of 'the stupid inertness of the puzzled negro…duller than that of an ox', he appropriated Ghanaian skills in axemanship: hacking through 'the densest primeval jungle and forest, without roads or paths of any kind to guard us'. The very emblem of the Boy Scout's kit that his dad had carried with pride, the Scout staff, was a design stolen from the forests of the Ashanti. 'Without a staff, one could not have got along at all' wrote Baden Powell.

Norman now detoured further forward in time and northwards in place to the Berlin Olympic Stadium in 1936, as Jesse Owens won medal after medal.

'Perhaps this is a non-violent means of direct action to teach Goodwin a lesson. This could be our Ashanti War or 1936 all over again,' whispered Norman seeking collusion with Michael, in a dreamy trance. Their mud-splattered backs were turned to Goodwin.

'You talk in riddles man, a translation would be helpful. I guess it could be fun.'

'No time for that Crozzy,' urged Norman converting historical ideals into pragmatic action, 'no time to waste.'

Turning back, with an affected casual air and shrugged shoulders, Norman replied, 'OK, just give us a few minutes to get a team together.'

'Better be faster than the take-aways round 'ere,' Goodwin guffawed as he nudged Euston to take his cue.

It took five minutes to conscript a reluctant Vikram, Chan, Rudzinski and several of Carozza's younger cousins to join them on the asphalt battlefield.

In Brookdale, the only balls permitted in the playground were of the tennis variety. Close skills were honed through this deprivation and Norman had forged similarities with Pele learning ginga with mangoes and grapefruit in the favela. Norman's tropical trance was broken by the cold drizzle that sprayed his forehead.

'Let's get this game going before the wet-play bell rings,' he urged his battalion.

When the 'game' started it became sickeningly clear to understand Goodwin's reasons for the match. Each time one of Norman's team got the rain-weary tennis ball, Goodwin and his team-mates chanted terrace-styled abuse.

'Come on Curry Muncher, pass it like you do the menu at your stinking Curry House.'

'Chinks can't play soccer, you can't see the ball with

those slanty eyes!'

As Norman shook the ball to rid it of water and smoothed back the loose yellow fur like a dog after its bath, he placed it for a corner kick. Goodwin rushed opposite him for marking duties and grinned at his team. 'Look lads, it's a Zebra crossing! Come on Oreo, what have you got?' Norman momentarily paused to admit the wit of Goodwin's pun before toe-punting the tennis ball towards the red-flushed face of Carozza.

The cross was greeted by Carozza's signature 'side of the head' flick, diving dramatically but narrowly missing the navy-blue jumper that had been bundled up and fashioned into a goalpost. He landed arms forward in asphalt grazing denial, a show of athleticism that garnered the respect of all onlookers.

As Goodwin retrieved the ball, he furtively checked Hemsway was out of earshot before commentating sardonically with an imaginary microphone in his hand, 'Too much grease on the ball, Spic, from your slimy hair. Just another I-Tie trying to be flash.'

Carozza burpied to his feet in a swift Cassock dancer motion and charged at the opposing team, only stopping at a stunned Goodwin. Like a domino, Goodwin was knocked over in an instant, tipped over by the pointing of Michael's fingertip to his chest.

'You boy, Carozza!' called Hemsway, affronted by the blatant challenge to his renowned stance on active playground vigilance. In his voice you could hear the cold calculation of a butcher weighing up the scales of fate, pausing before naming the price.

The other players froze in disbelief at the spooled slow-motion scene unravelling before them. Goodwin arose tentatively like a tightrope walker and feigned a wink to regain some playground credibility to no onlooker in particular. An attempt at a smirk crept to the edges of his mouth then withdrew, now alert to reality and ossified in a look of humiliation.

'Are you alright son?' enquired Hemsway, in clipped military tones more used to the imperative of commands rather than questions of customer service. 'Help him up boys, you'll be alright, no blood, no concussion.' Hemsway was no Mary Seacole, the British-Jamaican nurse and healer, famed for her altruism in the Crimean War. His bedside manner left plenty to be desired on the homely front.

As Goodwin was hauled up like a wounded soldier by two of his team, his mouth widened into a phoenix-like grin of realisation amid the flames of doubt.

'Straight to the headmaster's office Carozza!' signalled Hemsway, making a traffic policeman's signpost with his straightened arm and ominously pointing his index finger.

Carozza was still red with the rage of indignation; sweat mingled with what looked like tears. Hemsway frogmarched him, now shocked and pale-faced from the playground.

The score may have been nil-nil but it felt like an own goal to Norman.

That afternoon, Carozza's empty chair taunted Norman. A couple of Year 7 students had seen Mr and Mrs Carozza leaving the school with their shamefaced son. Word had spread that he had been suspended for a week.

In disbelief and shock, Norman ruminated on Carozza's act of martyrdom for Pan-Blandfordism. On reflection, Norman concluded that peaceful demonstrations would be far more effective than direct action.

CHAPTER TEN

Library Refugees

Without his ally, Norman felt disorientated. No man was an island, and Norman was no exception to the cliché.

Unanchored in the lonely expanse of the playground, Norman moored himself to the security of the library. Sheltered in its greenhouse of optimism, Norman read widely about the power of bus boycotts in the American Deep South, as he mentally transported himself from South Blandfordshire.

Sparked by the arrest of Rosa Parks on the 1st of December 1955, the Montgomery bus boycott was a thirteen-month mass protest, ending with the Supreme Court ruling that segregation on public buses was unconstitutional. Coordinated by the Montgomery Improvement Association, its President Martin Luther King, became a prominent Civil Rights leader and attracted international attention. To Norman's widening eyes, it was an instructive example of the potential of nonviolent mass protest. Norman hoped this seminal event in the US Civil Rights Movement could inspire his movement in Blandford, where Carozza's bold attempts had been thwarted.

Norman felt like his only friends were the Civil Rights

heroes whom he met for daily strategy meetings amidst Brookdale's dusty bookshelves. As Norman spent more time in the library, he noticed that several other 'minority groups' hung around there. To the left of the reference books, Norman saw Vikram and Chan hunched over a chessboard like security guards watching CCTV footage. There were a disproportionate number of other Chinese and Asian students. Norman recognised a few of Carozza's cousins at the computers as they talked to each other in a creole of Italian and English.

It suddenly dawned on Norman that he felt he was on a slowly sinking asylum boat, stranded between continents, like the ones he saw adrift in the Mediterranean near Lampedusa on the news. Norman and the others in similar straits had subconsciously smuggled themselves aboard to avoid the playground pecking order of casual racism. This was human trafficking of self-selection, for a level of subsistence available from exile. The parents of many of those in the library that lunchtime were originally political or economic migrants. But their children were still fleeing; only this time to the library, in their small numbers. Norman, self-appointed President of the yet-to-be-formalised Pan-Blandford Association, decided to do some ethnographic fieldwork, as a participant-observer.

'What brings you here guys?' he asked Chan and Vikram in expectant tones, eager to prove his hypothesis on minority displacement. They were deeply involved in a chess game. He whispered to avoid the attention of Mr Reed, who may have been timid but was a stickler for the 'appropriate noise levels' in the library. He would send students back, without ceremony, to the chaos of the playground for any violation of his strict decibel thresholds.

Chan continued to study the black and white board whilst Norman focused on their chequered lives. Both considered their next move as Chan's finger hovered over the pawn; a dragonfly above lily pad. Vikram raised his tangerine turbaned head. His bushy eyebrows, nervously surmounting his thick black-rimmed NHS-issued glasses, followed suit, struggling to separate like a novelty nose and glasses set from a joke shop. Vikram vacillated ambiguously between uber-chic and uber-geek. It was he, the bolder of the two players, who made the first move.

'Same as you probably, to avoid toss-pots like Goodwin.'

Norman was taken aback by Vikram's acerbity. He was so softly spoken and polite in class. Norman recoiled from the sting, feeling exposed in shared vulnerability with his research objects. Fully aware of this theoretical alliance with minorities, he now needed to embrace reality and practice solidarity. There was no room for ego in his vision of Pan-Blandfordism.

Recovering from his thoughts, Norman put his vanity aside and replied, 'Yes comrades. I could not agree more. I have a dream that soon we will be free at last, from tormentors like Goodwin who judge us by the colour of our skins, or where we are from, rather than the beauty of our minds, what is within.'

Chan let his pawn slip from his fingers, it rolled slowly from side to side in rhythmic and hypnotic retreat. He could only scratch his head in response to Norman's grandiose and eloquent oratory.

'Where did that speech come from Norman?' Chan jibed, partly in jest and partly in awe.

Norman basked in this fresh feeling of being heard as an equal, mesmerising his audience with the cadence of the Civil Rights movement; imparting his newly prized knowledge. Vikram and Chan were pawns in his hands, awaiting his strategic move. His evangelism was short-lived.

'To be honest Norman, I thought that you were more interested in Hip Hop and sport than cerebral affairs,' added Chan.

'And who said they are mutually exclusive interests?' rebuffed Norman in a bid to channel the mysticism of the proselytised.

Norman respected the boys' honesty, humour and intellect. He felt more at home in their extended family, where appearances were the poor cousins to ideas. Norman was liberated in the company of these free thinkers and the enlightenment of geek-chic. He concluded his conversation with Vikram and Chan in earnest fervour, 'Comrades, we are library refugees seeking asylum. We must unite and stand up against our oppressors. We must forge our own brand of Pan-Africanism: Pan-Blandfordism.'

His grand bubble was burst by the ever-pragmatic caution of Vikram's cold, rational logic, translating his emotive plea into a spreadsheet of cost/benefit analysis, 'So how do you propose we do that Norman? Use your fists and get suspended like Carozza?'

These were valid questions needing consideration. Norman knew he would need a Grandmaster's game plan, like those in Montgomery, to topple Goodwin and his pawns. He needed to convince Vikram, Chan and the silent minorities that risking the status quo would pay greater dividends than their shared failures in the current stock market.

'I'm working on it,' conceded Norman in a stalemate hastened by the bell that rang for the next lesson. Vikram and Chan sombrely swept up their chess pieces with their forearms.

After school Norman visited his erstwhile ally. He had often stood chatting at the uPVC framed frosted glass door of Carozza's house. But Norman had never gone in. He tiptoed tentatively up the elaborate, neatly-edged garden path, paving the way to the blonde-brick veneer of the 1960s semi-detached house. The brick was interrupted by a rectangular section of render where the coping stones had fallen off, like a bright alabaster shell stranded on the beach.

He rang the doorbell, imagining himself as a Roman messenger, the 'cursus publicus', humbled between two impressive plastic-moulded Corinthian columns. He had carefully tethered his chariot and horse, his Raleigh BMX, at the front gate as his hands fumbled with the combination lock. Since Michael had been suspended, Norman had cycled to school to hasten the lonely walk home.

The door was guarded by two white resin lions adorned with dreary Blandfordshire bird droppings. Through the layers of frosted glass bordered by ornate lace curtain, he could discern the substantial and blurred shape of Michael Carozza.

On the way there, Norman had texted:

'Crozzy, is it OK to pop round? Can't believe you got suspended. So sorry ☹'

He had found relief in the immediate response:

'Not your fault mate. Come around. Parents out, bored ☺'

To his surprise, the doorbell heralded the rousing sounds of strings, brass and cymbals that flourished into the Fratelli d'Italia. It was instantly recognisable to Norman's musical ear. The tune of the Brothers of Italy greeted the brothers of Pan Blandfordism.

The cymbals crashed, forcing the door open. Norman was welcomed in Mediterranean style with a bear hug and kisses on his left and right cheeks. Actions in this part of the world spoke more proudly than words.

'Hey, I recognised the tune on the doorbell, it's the Italian national anthem. It brings me back to your lucky World Cup final win! The car horns blared all night!' joked Norman.

'Spot on, gotta love the Il Canto degli Italiani!' enthused Michael, assuming an imaginary conductor's baton. 'It's so boring not being at school, I never thought I'd say that!' Carozza laughed. 'Come on,' he gestured, unfurling his arm like an over-attentive waiter. It was reassuring to see both his pride and sense of humour remained intact.

Norman hurriedly pressed down on the heels of his shoes as he noticed Michael's moccasins resting on a carpeted inversion of Michelangelo's cloud nine. He sunk into the firmament of the soft cream shag pile. It must have been recently shaken and vacuumed. It felt so much more luxurious than the worn Axminster in the Smith household, which frayed at the edges and had a leathery sheen that formed a mirage in the light of the day. Norman had, however, enjoyed its similarities to an ice rink when he was a little younger and more carefree.

Walking further into Michael's house, the smell of air freshener competed with tobacco fumes, wrestling within his nostrils for ascendancy, too evenly matched to declare a winner. Norman's eye travelled along the opulent golden wallpaper to the Artex-covered ceiling; roughly hewn circular clouds in a 1980s rendering of the Sistine Chapel. This was, however, a masterpiece completed by cowboy builders in 1988, not a master-craftsman in 1508. A cherub flew toward him and Cupid's arrow pierced him; he was in love with this place. His mind travelled back to the Roman Empire as he tried to conjure images of Gladiators competing with lions in the Colosseum.

In deference, Norman followed behind his guide. They entered a cluttered and ornate living room, quite unlike anything Norman had seen before. Faux mahogany display cabinets overflowed with china ornaments of Italian churches, clay countryside dioramas, crucifixes and decorous plates. On the top shelf, the plate of the Basilica di San Pietro stood to the left of centre stage: a picture, or rather an icon, of the Juventus player Del Piero.

Norman sank into an oversized black leather sofa next to his friend. At Michael's side of the couch lay anchored an open hemisphere lid of a sepia-rusted vintage bar globe. Norman navigated Design Toscano's 16th-century nautical map of the outside world, before marvelling at the view of the heavens that shone inside the lid. Within the globe rested a decadent crystal decanter and exotically spirited bottles of Limoncello, Anisette, Campari, Sambuca, Amaretto…sounding like remote islands off the coast of Sicily. Norman dreamt of supping these drinks in rhythm to the Mediterranean waves lapping his legs. It seemed a million miles from his father's puritanical and functional tallboy drinks cabinet, housing bland bottles of dry sherry. It left a sour taste of memory only marginally sweetened by the deep green label of Stone's Ginger wine added at Christmastide. The only highlight was the folding shelf. Cultures of restraint and ostentation collided and dizzied Norman's mind.

In characteristically laid-back style, Michael pulled a lever at the side of the sofa downwards and lowered the crankshaft of the sofa's sluice gate, like a lock keeper operating the sluice gates of the Grand Union Canal. His next button press unleashed a footrest as he interlocked his fingers to form a basket for his head, anticipating the ejection of the backrest and the reclining of the seat.

Norman paused, uncertain of whether to recount the recent playground incident.

Michael gazed upwards at the Artex gods in telepathic response. He quickly found his Delphic Sibyl for inspiration, pained with regret. 'I shouldn't have pushed him Norman. I know it won't help our chances in the future. It was just what that twerp Goodwin wanted.'

Norman was relieved he would not need to persuade Michael about the efficacy of non-violence as the modus operandi of Pan-Blandfordism. Carozza had come to this realisation on his own accord, through the expert tuition of bitter experience.

'I was angry at first,' continued Michael, his annoyance giving way to calmer philosophical tones, 'but I've had plenty of time on my own to think about what went down. Using my fists was just what Goodwin wanted. I'm the one who landed in trouble – not him. Did you see the smirk on his face when Hemsway came to his rescue?'

Recounting the incident heightened Michael and Norman's indignation but strengthened their resolve to even the score.

The Swiss-style cuckoo-clock ostentatiously announced four o'clock with a concomitant number of theatrically elongated clucks. Norman's stomach rumbled to signify it wasn't long before dinner. Come to think of it, with the excitement of his library fieldwork with Vikram and Chan, Norman realised he hadn't eaten his packed lunch. Not finishing the entire packed lunch was a transgression Norman's mother would find hard to forgive, not having had the luxury of three square meals in her village upbringing.

'I'm starving Croz, is it ok if I have my lunch here?'

'Of course, mate,' replied his friend looking on sympathetically and eyeing with suspicion his worst fears about the English palate. Norman apologetically extricated a peanut butter sandwich, thinly spread with a layer of margarine followed by a somehow thinner layer of peanut butter. The 'spread' was aptly sandwiched between the 'No Frills' brand of limp, multigrain bread. It was cost-cutting fare that made the customer digest their abstemious choices regretfully. Michael analysed the meagre cross-section with the concern of a geologist on a field trip.

'English food is not very inspiring, is it mate,' sighed Michael. 'Do you want some Parmesan?' Met by Norman's puzzled face, lips pursed to meet his peanut buttered fate, he checked himself quickly to translate, 'Parmesan cheese…to add some flavour?'

Confidently, without awaiting a response in true 'Mamma Mia knows best' style, Michael headed into the kitchen and returned triumphantly with a bowl of freshly shaven Parmesan cheese and a proud smile. He held it aloft like a gift from the Pantheon.

'We love food in Italy, it's an art form, the national obsession.' Michael, ever the showman, lowered the bowl of cheese and hovered his nose over it, welcoming the aroma with grand curlicues of his hands. His dramatic movement was concluded with a clichéd kissing of thumb and first four fingertips, forming a bilabially explosive and celebratory 'buono'. 'Sprinkle some of that gold dust on yer sarnie.'

As Norman savoured the newly discovered mixture of smooth and sweet peanut butter coalescing with the piquancy of Parmesan, he felt lucky that there were fusions in culture and that not everyone was as ignorant as Goodwin. A counter-plan, stimulated by his multi-cultured taste buds, was forming on the tip of Norman's tongue and fired the synapses of his hopeful, adolescent mind.

CHAPTER ELEVEN

The Pen is Mightier than the Sword

The week before, Ms Evens had some news, 'As you may or may not have guessed, I'll be on maternity leave from next week onwards, but you'll be in the capable hands of Mr Neal for the rest of the year.'

Ms Evens' optimistically delivered announcement had been met with pessimistic moans and groans from the class. Mr Neal, a supply teacher, was thought to be a dinosaur of education. He looked like Winston Churchill without the Homburg hat or cigar during school hours and wore a uniform of Harris Tweed even in summer. Where Ms Evens was avant-garde, Mr Neal was a traditionalist. Ms Evens favoured postmodern texts in contrast to Mr Neal's preference for the Classics. In the eyes of the majority of 10E inmates, the good cop was being replaced by the bad cop. English lessons were going to change melodramatically.

10E stirred listlessly in the corridor.

'Perhaps he's not coming after all,' hopefully whispered Norman to a newly reinstated Michael.

The anachronistic approach of brown brogues, Harris Tweed and briefcase confirmed their fears. Mr Neal strode past the snaking line and used his leather-patched elbow to prise open the door.

'My apologies Class 10E. Tardiness is a deadly sin but I was detained due to certain circumstances beyond my control. The bureaucratic Leviathan caught up with me...' The downward gesture of his hands, like an organist pressing down on airy keys, indicated it was time for the students to assume a sedentary position. Non-verbal cues were gratefully received by the class. Norman paused to consider issues of language variation and its evolution. He saw the irony of how Mr Line had attempted language immersion in French, but Mr Neal had mastered it in Old English.

Mr Neal rested his pigskin briefcase on his desk, took out a book and looked quizzically at the sea of puzzled expressions in front of him.

'Erm, to use the vernacular...I had to do some paperwork first, it is best to be honest. "Ah...No legacy is so rich as honesty". Shakespeare. My apologies 10E.'

From the back of the classroom came a monotonous humming. The fun and games were beginning. This was a stock standard passive-aggressive trick often successfully employed by Goodwin to ruffle the feathers of fledgling teachers. This, though, was not going to dissuade Mr Neal from stretching his wings.

'Whomever is humming this sonorous cacophony, at least something mellifluous would lighten the monotone somewhat.' Mr Neal spoke cheerfully and briskly, and this reaction caused collective consternation. Goodwin's lips froze. This was not part of the hackneyed script. The teachers usually, in keeping with the latest positive behaviour ethos, tactically ignored the humming and became noticeably more distracted and less able to teach, until they would snap, unfashionably, and shout at the class.

Norman was enchanted by Mr Neal in full flight, his ability to confuse students with his masterly use of language and poetic quotes, coupled with a theatrical presence. He reminded Norman of an older version of his dad. Now that the sideshow had been stopped, Mr Neal resumed his position centre stage.

'The golden age is before us, not behind us.'

'Shakespeare sir, I believe,' piped up Rudzinski.

'Indeed!' replied Mr Neal merrily before miming the doffing of his hat towards his interlocutor. Now with a broad sweep of his palm, Mr Neal addressed his captivated audience. 'Ladies and gentlemen, over the next few weeks, class, we will study the aforementioned master of our language, William Shakespeare. He was a wordsmith and played with words like your contemporary Hip Hop artists...' he paused for effect like a heavyweight boxer about to pull a knockout punch, '...Eminem and Dizzee Rascal.'

The last two references had, as Mr Neal planned, aroused the interest of the previously indifferent pointy end, unruly members of the class.

Norman was interested in both Hip Hop and language and wondered whether Shakespeare could be summoned to help him silence his critics as Mr Neal had just done so effectively. He thought back to the allusion to Richard III that Martin Luther King had used in his famous speech.

Mr Neal began to sketch his outline, 'We will be Shakespeare's apprentices. By means of an introduction, we will start our peregrinations by looking at one of Shakespeare's most famous plays, Othello. It concerns itself with universal themes that affect us as much now as they did in 1603 when it was believed to have been written; themes of racism, love, jealousy, betrayal, revenge and repentance.' At the mention of the words, 'racism' and 'revenge', Norman and Michael exchanged excited and knowing glances. 'I am aware that Ms Evens has been focusing on similar themes with different literature this term.' Norman shuddered at the memory of the Omo DVD.

As the lesson unfolded and the class read the first few scenes, Mr Neal supplied a wealth of background information about the central characters: Othello, 'the Moor', an African general in the Venetian army and Iago, Othello's manipulating ensign.

To aid comprehension of the class, Mr Neal offered a translation.

'The action begins in a street in Venice, in the middle of an argument between Roderigo, a rich man, and Iago. Roderigo has been paying Iago to help him marry his love, Desdemona. Dramatically, Roderigo has just learned that Desdemona has married Othello. Iago says he hates Othello, who recently gave the promotion of lieutenant to an inexperienced soldier named Cassio. Unseen, Iago and Roderigo cry out to Brabantio that his daughter Desdemona has been stolen by and married to Othello "the Moor"'.

Instantly, Norman became obsessed with the play. He became 'the Moor of Blandford' battling against Goodwin as Iago. The scene was acted out clumsily by selected students before Mr Neal once again wove the narrative threads together.

'Brabantio finds that his daughter is indeed missing, and he gathers some officers to find Othello. A master of deceit, Iago, not wanting his hatred of Othello to be known, leaves Roderigo and hurries back to Othello before Brabantio sees him.'

Norman was left on the edge of his seat.

'Our reading will, I hope, inspire our writing. To guide us and satisfy the assessment gods, I propose a group presentation task. I must, as your teacher, be cruel to be kind. The assessment task is to explain how the pen is mightier than the sword.' Mr Neal, as he was prone to when excited, offered a quotation to provide a footnote, 'In Hamlet, 1602 if my memory serves me correctly, Shakespeare gave Rosencrantz the line … "many wearing rapiers are afraid of goose-quills and dare scarce come thither." The rapier is the sword and the goose-quill the pen, listeners.'

Reading the mystified expressions masquerading as politeness worn by the class, Mr Neal realised his charges needed more practical detail.

'It has to be delivered in front of the whole of the Upper School – Years 7 to 12, to add dramatic tension. In groups of three or four, you may elect your colleagues in this project. Form your own interest groups.' Mr Neal sighed then repeated his mantra, 'Alas, I must be cruel, only to be kind.'

Norman began to see an opportunity as he watched Goodwin squirm in his seat. It had been quite the revelation last year when Goodwin had uncharacteristically revealed his Achilles heel. Although ready with humiliating banter, Goodwin had shown how uncomfortable he was with formal public speaking. In both debating tasks and the ten-minute presentation, Goodwin had shaken with a genuine fear which his classmates had initially interpreted as sarcasm. The class had looked on with discomfort and disbelief whilst Goodwin stumbled on his tongue, a diminutive voice wavering as if he were ordering food in an unfamiliar language. He had swayed from side to side like a pendulum deciding his fate. Goodwin had recovered skilfully and maintained street credibility by deriding public speaking as nerdy.

The bell rang as if on cue and Mr Neal, once more, employed a quote to acknowledge the end of the lesson. "Like as waves make towards, the pebbl'd shore, so do our minutes, hasten to their end." I look forward to working alongside you 10E.' With that, Mr Neal abruptly stood up, turned on his heels, put his interleaved and dog-eared copy of Othello into his briefcase and left, ignoring the Workplace Health and Safety directive that students should leave first. Bemused and intrigued in equal parts, measure for measure, the class, accustomed to pushing their way out of Ms Evens' class, sheepishly followed their shepherd.

CHAPTER TWELVE

Nicked Names

Straight after their eccentric dismissal, Norman ambitiously arrested himself from the collective shock and seized his opportunity. Walking with Michael, he quickened his pace to catch up with Vikram and Chan. Lunging forward to tap Vikram on his shoulder like a batsman clambering for his crease, he spoke seriously in a hushed voice, 'Let's meet in the library at lunchtime. I think I have a plan.'

Before Vikram could answer, Goodwin sauntered past with Steve Euston following deferentially. 'Well, if it ain't the United Nations of Pakis, Chinks and I-Ties! And to cap it off, Oreo!' jeered Goodwin as he continued on his merry way.

'We'll be there,' responded Vikram as spokesman for the pair. He seemed to be answering both Norman and Goodwin at once, although the antagonist and his assistant were out of earshot with their backs turned, swaying in a highly stylised act of corridor braggadocio.

'What's happening Norman, what's the plan?' peevishly quizzed Michael.

'Can't explain now. No time. You can't be late for your next lesson. You're on report remember and we need you at school for this. See you all at lunchtime in the library.'

One of the conditions of Michael's return to school had involved the signing of a behaviour 'contract' which each teacher had to sign. Punctuality was the first criteria or 'target' for each lesson.

The following lesson crawled by as Michael, Vikram and Chan struggled to concentrate, waiting impatiently for the bell to ring. Norman continued to be distracted by a lesson tangent that Mr Neal had got onto earlier in the week, when he had become animated about the origins of symbolic culture and language. The words rang once more in his ears. 'For words to have power, for "x" to mean "y", they must be invested with the most vital human quality of them all, trust…"x", "y", "trust".'

Norman again considered that the word 'omo' only had the meaning that a group of people agreed to; part of a social contract, lubricated and actualised by trust. 'Omo' could be a detergent, a racist insult or the word for a child. He knew intimately and painfully of this process, of the meanings invested in by Goodwin and his ilk for 'Oreo', 'Zebra' and 'Bounty'. Words were neither in stasis nor monolithic.

Like blacksmiths forging ahead, bending and shaping metal, words could be reformed, repurposed, rearranged, reinvented, reclaimed and refashioned to suit the craftsperson and their audience. Shakespeare came to his mind with his reputation as a wordsmith and firebrand. New meanings were possible, new openings in linguistic labyrinths.

Norman thought of the word 'nigger' and its historically oppressive echoes, how it was imbued with that special force and viciousness. It had a power of momentum, like a runaway truck over time, accumulating the might of authority through its repetition. When uttered by Goodwin, it was as if he joined the voices of all the taunts of the past. At once it linked him to the slave master and the Klu Klux Klan. Much to his delight though, the word had been re-appropriated as 'nigga' by Hip Hop artists.

In solidarity, an increasing number of people had stood by this new term and seized ownership of it. 'Niggers' were empowered as 'niggas'. It took its own epithet and threw it back at society. The gamble of flaunting the name had been worth it, the meaning had changed and made it a badge of honour rather than an insult; trash transformed into treasure. 'For "x" to mean "y", words had to be invested with trust' became a mantra playing on a loop in Norman's mind.

At the library, Norman waited eagerly for the other 'nations' to arrive for their meeting.

'Wassup my comrades!?'

'Cut the crap Norman – what's the big idea?'

'Well Vikram, let's just say I'm developing an idea for the group presentation task for Neal. Are you guys in? We could form a group.'

'Like the United Nations!' joked Michael.

'That's not such a crazy idea,' replied Norman earnestly.

The other boys were intrigued at how serious and focused their Chairperson had become.

'Before that though, I need some material – let's call it research or fieldwork.'

'You've been watching too much National Geographic,' quipped Chan to everyone's amusement, including Norman's.

'Very good Chan. We will need our wits about us, or at least our wit in this campaign. Anyway, let's get started.'

Norman punctuated the end of theorizing and the start of action by pressing on the end of his ballpoint pen with his thumb to release its nib, like medicine ejected from a syringe. He leaned forward in his chair and with his left hand withdrew a brand-new notebook, courtesy of Sandeep's Corner Store, from his left trouser back pocket as if he were a classy waiter or a musketeer in a dual.

'I'll have a Coke please,' giggled Vikram as the others joined in, momentarily releasing the valve of tension.

'All jokes aside comrades, which 'nicknames' do you find most offensive? Humour me,' probed Norman mischievously, buoyed by the promise of irony.

'Well, I'm not a big fan of, let me see, "Chinky", "Ching Chong Chinaman", "Slanty-eyes", "Slope', or "Nip" for that matter.'

Norman furiously wrote down these insults under the heading "Nicked Names", underscoring the importance with two dramatic lines. In a curious role reversal, Norman, who frequently proofread and edited Michael's essays of late, was corrected by his understudy. 'Norman, you don't need the -ed, or the space between the words, it's just nicknames.'

'Forsooth, but Carozza, these 'nicknames' have been taken from us – nicked, so to speak, so they are nicked names.' Vikram and Chan smiled appreciatively at the play on words whilst Michael looked like he was still trying to work it out.

'Your turn Vikram.'

'Where do I start? Well 'Paki', 'Curry Muncher' or anything about curry, it's all offensive. I'm from Sylhet, eastern Bangladesh, in actual fact. I wish people such as Goodwin could at least insult me accurately, such laziness!' Vikram wrote the word Sylhet in the Sylheti-Nagri alphabet. A horizontal bar from which hung magical runes and hieroglyphs, to elaborately prove his point.

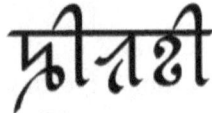

'Likewise,' added Chan, feeding on this last supper of shared indignation, 'Nip, in fact, refers to Nippon, Japan, not China. If only these muppets knew something of the complex history of Sino-Japanese relations, or of the partitioning of India for that matter!'

Chan drew something that looked like a ladder.
'This is kanji for sun or day.'

He repeated the ladder shape and then added symbols to the right of it.

'This means clear, bright. And this means gloomy.'

'Notice how the first element, relating to the image of the ladder to the sun is developed to produce new meanings?'

His comrades looked on in awe.

'Kanji developed from pictures used by us Chinese several thousand years ago to represent the world around us. Many of the symbols though have become very abstract. In addition, the Japanese use two other phonetic alphabets, cursive hiragana for words not written in kanji, verb endings and parts of speech as well as angular katakana. Katakana is used for emphasis and to write words and names not of Chinese and Japanese origin.

See, this represents Nihon, or Japan. The main element, as you can see, is sun combined to the right with hon, origin.'

'Aha, Nippon and Nihon literally mean "the sun's origin, the Land of the Rising Sun",' beamed Norman, his head aglow with enlightenment.

'Spot on Norman,' grinned Chan in reply.

Norman thought about the might of the pen, the beautiful calligraphy of Arabic, Sinhalese, kanji, Twi letters and in the case of Viking runes, a sword penned the words. The words were made by the pen of a sword. He was giddy with these new connections.

Norman could relate to misnomers too. 'Don't worry, half the time people don't know where I'm from, so I get a whole lot of names; Paki, I-Tie, Chink, Golliwog, Jungle Bunny; you name it, I've been called it.' The others nodded in unison.

'To conclude, Crozzy, what's on your hit list?'

'You know, Spic, Dago, I-Tie, Pizza Boy. They can call me the Italian Stallion though!'

Listening to each nicked name had given them unexpected confidence and sense of purpose. Saying the words themselves and then writing those down seemed to diminish their power.

'Well my niggas, that was very useful,' concluded Norman, absent-mindedly. Registering his schoolmates' surprise he elaborated. 'Look, by saying these words ourselves, we are beginning to take ownership of them. Just like NWA took ownership of the 'n-word'. Norman wrote the word 'nigger' provocatively, paused then crossed it out flamboyantly before replacing it with 'nigga' beside it in his notebook. 'These nicked names have been stolen from us, and so we must take them back, one insult by one. An I-Tie for an I-Tie!'

'But how does this fit into the group presentation?'

'Don't worry Vikram – it will,' grinned Norman as he put his notebook and pen in his back pocket.

'I'm starving,' complained Chan. The end-of-lunch bell rang in confirmation of his hunger pangs. The allies quickly grabbed their bags, denying their rumbling stomachs, to ensure they wouldn't be late for their next classes.

As they ran down the navy-blue carpeted corridor, fuelled with adrenaline, neither Norman nor his friends noticed the soft thud of his notebook fall out of his back pocket, brushed by Michael's bag as he swung it onto his shoulder like a hammer thrower gaining momentum.

On his way to class from a lunchtime 'reflection' (the euphemism for detention coined by the Department of Education), Goodwin saw a white buoy floating conspicuously on the blue carpet. As he got closer Goodwin saw that it was a spiral-bound A5 notebook. Stooping for closer inspection, he turned it over and saw 'Norman Smith 10E' written on it. He instinctively swept it up with glee, in a gymnastic three hundred and sixty degrees turn to see that no-one had spotted him. He stood up, proud of his achievement, to the imagined applause of his fawning audience.

Nicked Names

Chan:	Chinky, Ching-Chong Chinaman, Slanty Eyes, Slope, Nip
Vikram:	Paki, Curry Muncher
Michael:	Spic, Dago, I-Tie, Pizza Boy

This first and only entry in the notebook made for intriguing reading. Goodwin salivated as he read over the list of names and epithets. In his hunger, Goodwin hadn't noticed the '-ed' in the title.

In the canteen, in the dying minutes of the ephemeral afternoon break, Goodwin rushed towards Norman as he waited for the vending machine to splutter out his hot chocolate.

'What does that loser want?' whispered Chan to Vikram and Michael, further back in the queue. Goodwin jeered at Norman and held the notebook aloft as if he were brandishing a hard-fought soccer trophy. 'Oi, Zebra, something of yours I do believe!'

Norman felt a sinking feeling. Part of his plan was in Goodwin's hands. He needed to play it cool and not show his panic. 'Oh, yeah…must've dropped it. Thanks.'

'Now let me see. It was quite an interesting read Oreo. Never thought you had it in you!' Goodwin flicked slowly through the pages; savouring his power to make Norman wait.

'Could I just have it please? I've got to go to Science, you know what Hemsway is like if you're late…'

'Plenty of time, Bounty Boy. Let's do some English work instead. Let's see,' Goodwin paused on a page, his eyes bright with excitement. 'Chinky – see,' he said pointing to Norman's rough notes, 'Paki…I-Tie…finally you've realised that your group are ethnic losers!'

'Well, er…' Norman had to think quickly. Goodwin hadn't worked out why Norman had written the names down. He would have to grin and bear it, bite his lip whilst Goodwin mocked his friends. This was at least better than letting their tormentor find out their plan.

'Come on now Zebra. Don't be shy. Here's the proof. Ethnic losers, your mates. Even you admit it! Wait till Chan the Chink and Vikram the Paki find out what you really think of them!'

'Okay. Jus' give it back.'

'Even a half-caste like you can work it out. Mus' be the right half of your brain that sussed out what a useless team you have,' chuckled Goodwin to himself, pleased with his play on words.

If Norman could let this storm pass, then he would be able to play with the 'nicked names' in the notebook and get revenge. 'OK, OK. You're right. Notebook please, I'm in a hurry.'

'Curry Muncher in a hurry! Typical Paki you are! Pakis outnumbered 10 to 1!'

It was a familiar and disappointing chant to Norman. Goodwin often alternated teasing Norman as 'Zebra', 'Bounty' or 'Oreo' with 'Paki'. Did Goodwin realise that this was inconsistent and inaccurate? It was safer just to think of something else and let Goodwin's hot air evaporate. Norman was getting better at this, especially after seeing the failure of Michael's direct action. Goodwin was on cloud nine in his hot air balloon at that moment. Be patient, thought Norman, let

Goodwin have his moment of glory. Before long, if everything went according to plan, his nemesis would be crashing and burning in front of an audience.

Norman continued to enjoy English lessons with Mr Neal as the plot of Othello unfolded further. Each morning on his paper round, Norman listened to Hip Hop but also thought of the nicked names, the tautological torture and trauma, the irony of Goodwin stealing the notebook. Mr Neal's unintended mantra continued to pervade his thoughts 'for "x" to mean "y", words have to be invested in trust'.

The ideas came in short phrases. Each time they came to him, he wrote them down in his replacement A3 Art pad; he was determined that this book wouldn't slip out of his hands or back pocket. Ideas came to him throughout the day and night. It accompanied him in his paper round bag and he frequently checked it was at the bottom of his pile of exercise books during school hours.

'Norman, what are you doing?' asked Sandeep one morning, looking over his shoulder, as he scrawled in it, possessed by poetry. 'You are supposed to be marking the newspapers. I pay you to deliver papers, not poetry!'

'Sorry, Sandeep,' Norman replied as he wrote the end of the line that had just jumped into his mind. He returned to the prosaic task of writing house numbers and street names above the sticky ink of newspaper mastheads, in shorthand, in preparation for his daily deliveries.

'This must be a great project,' mused his father that evening, as he noticed his son once more head-deep in the Artist's pad.

CHAPTER THIRTEEN

Word Play

The day of the presentation had arrived. Norman woke with a calm feeling.

The whole of the Upper School had gathered as a mixture of anticipation and nervous excitement buzzed, like a swarm of flies in the darkened auditorium. The students now faced the reality of being put in the limelight, either to sink or swim in front of their peers.

To add to the dramatic tension, Mr Neal had arranged kettle drums to the left of the stage, with their bronze shining on the podium. The instruments, borrowed from the Music Department, were positioned to supply percussive shock therapy to accompany the introduction of each Act. Theatrical Studies and stagecraft for maximum effect were a forte of Mr Neal.

Norman's mind travelled back in time, imagining himself as a brave Christian in the Colosseum. He felt like he was always being pushed into the spotlight of Goodwin's spontaneous interrogations, so was at ease with the well-orchestrated limelight of the stage before him.

Goodwin, on the other hand, was visibly shaken. He tapped his foot awkwardly to an imaginary Techno soundtrack and his jawline chewed gum metronomically to the BPMs pulsating in his head.

The burgundy crushed-velvet curtains parted to reveal a bespectacled Mr Neal wearing a three-piece Harris Tweed and red bow-tie, centre stage under the banner 'The Pen is Mightier than the Sword'. He was uncharacteristically brief but nevertheless dramatic in his introduction. 'Let us do verbal battle, badinage, if you will.' Mr Neal paused like a pugilist before throwing the audience the punchline. The final blow was provided, to deliver the knockout.

'The swordplay of wordplay is all yours and awaits your applause!'

The first group presentation was a rather avant-garde skit, whereby two students dressed as a pen and sword respectively, recited the advantages of their relative prowess. The participants appeared to have prioritised their time in producing impressive costumes rather than working on the script. The pen, predictably more incisive, emerged as the moral winner over a bloodthirsty sword. Applause was polite though, as the students realised how hard it might be to succeed in this maverick assessment task.

A series of lacklustre presentations followed before the showstoppers. Goodwin's group included a nervous cast of his cronies, with Steve Euston sweating alongside them. They stumbled through a jingoistic speech about 'Why Blandford FC is a mighty team'. No references were made to a pen or a sword and these rudimentary omissions were registered in Mr Neal's furrowed brow. It was clear for all to see that the group were getting instant feedback in the form of their teacher's facial marking.

The 'speech' reached its diminuendo when Goodwin and his henchmen half-heartedly, but with bodies fully embarrassed, chanted weakly 'Blandford FC, pride of Blandford, two World Wars and one County Cup.' Their heads hung limply, as they swayed uncertainly, in pilloried shame under the weight of their red and white Blandford Football Club scarves.

The audience, many familiar with seeing Goodwin and his gang in control, sensed the momentous extent of their humiliation. Stunned silence gave way to tentative sniggers, evolving within seconds into the braver laughter of pairs, then groups, then whole rows until the auditorium erupted and shook with hysterical howling.

This self-sabotage was just the warm-up Norman had wanted as he set his sights on adding verbal insults to Goodwin's injuries.

The summoning of the kettle drums rumbled in time with Norman's heartbeat of nervous excitement. He was followed down the steps of Row F by Chan, Vikram, Michael and a late addition, Alan Rudzinski. He hadn't told the rest of the crew what he planned to do for fear they would not go through with it if they had time to think.

Norman announced their presence on stage, seizing the microphone from Mr Neal, who responded with a raising of eyebrows in salute to his dramatic assertiveness.

'Comrades. We have a dream - that the pen is mightier than the sword of our tormentors. Here's one for the bullies.'

Norman initiated a chain reaction, signalling for Chan to drop the needle to the backing record primed on the turntable. Chan answered by scratching to release a hypnotic trip-hop bassline. The audience responded by lurching their necks in time.

'Introducing the United Nations of Word Play.' Nodding to Chan, Norman dropped the first line:

'We are the Chink in your armour
Our penmanship will harm ya'

Chan began to grin as the plan unravelled one bar at a time.

'Eyes slanted in defiance – no compromise
To your droopy lies
We'll nip in between your schemes of violence
The UN of Word Play is on your side
Our pen is mightier than the sword.'

The audience was beginning to hear and appreciate the lyrical audacity on display.

Feeling the buzz of acknowledgment and support, Norman became broader in his swagger towards Alan. As Chan's bassline conditioned the crowd waiting for the next verse, Norman put the mic to his side and gave Alan a piece of paper cut neatly from his Art pad. 'Bro', just read this out in time with the beat then pass it on,' whispered Norman, microphone muted on his cheek.

He passed the baton to Alan and he ran with it,

'Even though we may be Poles apart
Beneath the surface we really aren't,'

The audience and the crew onstage nodded appreciatively in time and beckoned for more.

'Rudzinski slalom navigator swerving insults
Downhill expert, full speed ahead
Chopping beats like a delicatessen
In my Polski Sklep I'll teach you a lesson
The UN of Word Play is all yours
Our pen is mightier than the sword,'

Alan smiled widely and passed the paper and mic to Vikram, who smirked as he skimmed over his lines in advance, nodding to Chan's beats, the sellotape which held the rapping together. Vikram waited for two more loops, playing with the crowd's excitement, before unleashing his electrifying lines with aplomb:

'Pakis outnumbered ten to one
No son, you got it wrong
We give spice to the lifeless, bland and mealy-mouthed

Curry Munchers with fire to burn out your punches
Set you alight with turmeric, cumin and masala
Always on red alert to ignite ya
The UN of Word Play, angry child of divorce
Our pen is mightier than the sword'

This time the last line of the chorus was joined in force by his friends on stage and could be heard in the audience. Vikram grinned at Michael, high-fived him and passed the paper; no further introduction needed. Michael and Vikram, side by side, both bent their knees, buckled by the weight of the hypnotic bassline.

'Spic, Dago, I-Tie, heard it all before
Before you join in the chorus, I'll give you some more
I-tie you up in Latinate knots
You have no idea of the remedies I've got
My language Romances unties your Anglo-Saxon shackles
Unleashing lyrical laxatives
To your constipated consonant clusters
What's the matter, you're looking flustered?
Spic and span, I'll dress you down
Not a day goes by without cowardly lies
The UN of Word plays on your mind,'

The audience took Michael's invitation and jubilantly chorused:

'Our pen is mightier than the sword.'

Michael passed the microphone to Norman. He looked up and saw his dream was being realised. Norman pointed to himself with the microphone.

'This is Zebra crossing over the black and white borders
Towards a richer, more colourful chorus
I've never seen a person white or black
Millions of shades in between
That's the fact
A treasure chest brimming with bounty
Stand proud, Blandford is a multicultural county
The UN of Word Play, one more time for the chorus
Sing in one voice!'

In anticipation of the final chorus, the students of the Upper School stood up and swayed, hands in the air, one strong and unified force:

'Our pen is mightier than the sword!'

Goodwin was the only one still sitting down. The bombastic standing ovation finally brought him to his uncertain feet, fearful of what would happen if he didn't join in the celebration.

CHAPTER FOURTEEN

Funny Business Card

Norman spent the weekend coming back down to earth. Several congratulatory texts had been exchanged between the rap battle heroes over the last few days. Snap streaks of smileys and celebratory emojis peppered their screens. Norman's dad listened proudly to his son's animated recount, dubbing them as 'Blandford's sharp-tongued, poisonous pen poets.'

Over the next two weeks at school, strange things happened.

On Monday morning the industrial buzzer signalled that the workhouse treadmill was back in motion. Norman joined the throng who tucked in shirt tails, removed eyeliner, adjusted pleated skirts to regulation length and tightened school tie nooses decorated in diagonally striped royal blue and yellow hues.

'C'mon, on yer way. Let's be having you!' urged Hemsway as he glanced at his invisible watch that read melodrama o'clock. He looked like a caffeine-deprived lollipop man with the stick to stir, but without the cappuccino to sweeten the start of the week. Waving the latecomers into the gates of fortress education, cold air curlicues rose from his flared dragon's nostrils atop his cavalier moustache. Norman followed the ethereal wisps upward until his eyes met a murmuration of starlings, who gave Hemsway a 'V for Victory' sign. His head really was on cloud nine.

Norman traversed the threshold still replaying the glory of the previous week's performance, applause ringing in his ears. He ascended the worn blue carpeted stairs to his locker with an extra spring in his airy Doc Martens soles. Was it just him or were more people smiling and waving hello?

On autopilot, he swung his rucksack off his right shoulder in one fell swoop between his legs; the muscle memory of an axe-wielding lumberjack, a hammer thrower in reverse. His bag sat perched on his toes, nuzzling the lower laces of eight eyelets like the offspring of an Emperor penguin protected from hostile conditions, whilst Norman started to forage. At once he was part of a shifting huddle of bomber jackets, duffel coats, snorkels and parkas, swaying side to side, liberating and jettisoning stockpiled items from lockers in preparation for the day. The gunmetal grey flap swung open, freeing three horizontal gills at the bottom, perhaps breathing holes for half-forgotten mouldy food scraps secreted between books.

The second buzzer sounded to signal registration for tutor groups. As Norman gazed at his collage of photocopied images of Martin Luther King, Jesse Owens, William Shakespeare and Giddy Vandal, mic in hand, a smile crept from the edges of his lips.

Suddenly Norman froze. His daze was broken by the mysterious hushed harmonies and dulcet decibels of Goodwin talking to Steve Euston. He detected a certain restraint from the usual Punch and Judy show; gone was the sit-com delivery, canned laughter and applause.

'I just need to get some'ink from me locker. See you in English,' explained Euston as he continued his pigeon pattering steps away from them. Sensing Goodwin was getting closer, Norman spun around, a hammer thrower in second phase, to meet his nemesis, whose quivering dark monobrow ends raised themselves like a great horned owl's supercilium. Goodwin's signature snarl lay predictably beneath.

'Here's the deal...' Goodwin offered as an opening gambit, through the begrudging semi-clenched teeth of a constipated ventriloquist. Pausing, the periscope of Goodwin's neck extended and looked side to side. Norman held his stoic silence, waiting for the customary syntactical closure of 'Zebra', however nothing was forthcoming. Goodwin lowered his voice a notch, 'My boys'll leave you and your nerdy freak show alone as long as you lot don't harp on about last week.'

Punctuation came in the form not of a punchline, but rather a sharp poke on Norman's pre-pubescent right pectoral. Pectoralis major Norman mouthed sotto voce, his lips reminiscing in synchrony. His head nodded slowly, over a rare, interesting moment in a PE Theory lesson the other week. Why did Latinate terms sound so commanding and alluring?

It began to sink in, the realisation of Goodwin's begrudging acceptance. Could this really have just happened?

Then, on Wednesday in Food Technology, something more than the ingredients turned, thawed and defrosted under the power of the Brookdale radiators and microwaves. 10F listened politely to Mrs Hemsway deliver the perfunctory health, safety and hygiene precursor to the practical lesson as she twisted and stretched her dirty, dyed blonde-tipped perm to the corner of her lips. Goodwin rolled his eyes towards Norman in what could only be described as a look of solidarity.

Shortly afterwards, upon their release to the clinical zinc-topped counters, Norman sprinkled his wooden chopping board and rolling pin gingerly with all-purpose white flour in preparation for puff pastry. Meanwhile, at the benchtop directly opposite, Goodwin puffed out his chest in his own preparations. Assuming the role of Tarzan, he attacked a chicken breast with a metal meat mallet, much to Norman's unexpected amusement. Having never previously witnessed any of Goodwin's talents, it was perhaps not just the chicken that was being tenderised by these unconventionally brash ways.

The tail end of the school week drifted along in a satisfying rhythm, like the unfettered twin lobes of a perch's caudal fin in the Grand Union Canal. Norman enjoyed the odd soccer game with Michael as well as regular library visits to catch up with Vikram and Chan.

Mr Neal never did return to give the students their official assessment results. Instead, Mr Jones, one in a lacklustre line of successive supply teachers who attempted to contain 10E, delivered them the following Friday afternoon.

'The moment you have been waiting for. Mr Neal has kindly marked these. Above and beyond if you ask me.'

'We didn't ask you for your evaluation of Mr Neal's marking sir,' retorted Alan Rudzinski to nerve-assuaging chuckles. As the year was ending, coursework results had assumed more gravity than the heady halcyon days at the start of the term.

'I believe he's started some publishing venture or other, so you may not have the pleasure again any time soon.' Mr Jones began to dish out the papers, cutting through the stunned silent air to meet eager hands. Next, it was Norman's turn. Mr Jones stood above him, holding Norman's red, plastic wallet file kept in place with a black elastic tie.

Norman's stomach flipped a gymnastic perfect ten in recognition. He was going to miss Mr Neal: the unexpected tangents and guidance; gifts delivered in double periods, wrapped up in Harris Tweed, brogues and a leather briefcase. His mind continued to oscillate on the asymmetrical bars of future obstacles;

impediments he would have to navigate without his master. Norman was brought back to an anecdote Mr Neal had told the class about the power of visualisation. Back in the 80s, a famous Russian Olympic coach had caused a sensation by insisting that his squad sat and meditated before enacting their routines. Neurologists had proved that this act of the imagination helped lay down pathways in the brain that increased the likelihood of success. Breathing deeply, Norman closed his eyes in a bid for gold and hoped for the best. He gulped down extra air to fortify his dreams.

Norman met Mr Jones's offer of the red A4 document file halfway and swiftly pressed it against his rapidly beating chest. He pulled the elastic band aside to reveal his fate, his clammy palm stuck to the triangle of the file as he popped open the seal flap with his left thumb. He whisked out the assessment task, the umbilical cord to his former mentor. Norman scanned the first page, his eyes moving across a black sea of ticks, sodium welling in his tear ducts, and floating momentarily on encouraging angular annotations like 'indeed', 'insightful point', 'powerful imagery' and the like. With a straight angled twist of his left wrist, Norman turned the stapled papers over in the manner of an expert croupier.

Dear Norman,

You supplied your audience with a veritable lyrical and lexical treasure chest. Your pen has *proved to be a mighty instrument indeed. Your ability to coin phrases, borrow and adapt words, is in the same vein as the great man himself, William Shakespeare (his being predominantly a Latin and Germanic substrate, yours a rich aggregate of Blandford, Leestone and MLE as my sociolinguistics reading informs me!).*

Overall Grade: A

His heart recovered to a steadier beat as endorphins diluted adrenaline. A natural reward. Norman savoured Mr Neal's words, forwards and backwards, mouthing the words bilabially, tasting a fine Ribena. Stapled to the bottom was a business card:

Neal Publishing Services

Editing, proof-reading, typesetting
Printing, publishing & distributing
Marketing & Public Relations
Book Tours and Author Events
Mr Geoffrey Peter Neal
nealnerd1@imail.com

As Norman turned the card, he caught sight of Mr Neal's handwriting on the back. He eagerly deciphered the postscript.

May you continue to use your pen to the power of goodness. Continue to ink your imagination Norman.

Do keep in touch.

Mr Neal

Home Tel (01524) 372903 / Mob. +447700 900796

EPILOGUE

These days Norman preferred to dictate or 'spit' his lyrics into his smartphone. He would then decide, in consultation with his producer, manager and publicity agent, whether a soundtrack was befitting for the occasion.

In his airy Hoxton studio, Norman prepared his voice. This area, the formerly self-effacing ghetto, was now over-inflated in ego and rent. He swayed in time to the stifled moans of the nearby underground trains, regular as their timetables. The carriages wheezed and sighed, opening their doors to allow the gentrified to pass in and out. At times he felt a long way from his Blandfordshire childhood.

Norman was an acclaimed Renaissance Man. A recent magazine article had celebrated him as 'a multi-hyphenate creative originally from the Home Counties. Norman Z.E.B.R.A is the rapper, poet and artist exploding your headphones with music that confronts issues of race, identity and politics. Born Norman Smith, Zebra's electric performances set crowds ablaze when he's on stage, spitting on weighty issues to an audience with a palpable connection to this socially conscious artist.'

The article went on to applaud his experimental sound and achievements: 'Having started an English Literature degree at Gonville and Caius College,

Cambridge, he quit his study halfway to concentrate on music at Leestone College of Performing Arts, before going on to become the capital's hottest new musical talent. We caught up with the artist to discuss inspirations, his High School English teacher turned agent and why his parents are his heroes.'

He thought back to Blandford and again felt the familiar glow produced by the embers of lyrics coming to him, just like they used to on his newspaper round.

The Writing on the Wall

'Wogs out' the graffiti sprayed
In those Blandfordshire days
That led me to question
With what affection
was my sort held?

Signed 'National Front' in marker pen iridescence
On pallid South Blands Council urinals
Indecencies scrawled indelibly
On my mind
That led me to question
With what affection
was my sort held?

The shards of corner shop glass
Thwarted our fragile path
To post-racial harmony
We lived in the Dark decades
Ages
of ignorance and violence

Was it my problem?
That the chant was sung:
'Pakis outnumbered 10 to 1'
That led me to question
With what affection
was my sort held?

In morbid expectation
I awaited black History pages
Of dehumanised victims

Beads of perspiration created
A red glow of knowing tinged my skin
As I uncomfortably listened in
to narratives
of the passive recipients of slavery
Tragedies with no heroes
That led me to question
With what affection
was my sort held?

In contemplation
Was it your intention?
For me to assent to
Condescending classifications
And ideas of Nation?

Racism was never mentioned
In those Blandfordshire...

His doorbell buzzed and he regained composure to recite the last line in full.

In those Blandfordshire days.

Norman rushed to the intercom.

'X stands for Y my boy!'

'Ah, Geoffrey! Do come up.'

www.ingramcontent.com/pod-product-compliance
Lightning Source LLC
Chambersburg PA
CBHW030232180626
46810CB00008B/3095